'I find it sad and very dangerous for the girls and for their clients, especially now there is AIDS.' Michiel shrugged. 'It is the oldest profession and we found cures for most of the venereal diseases and now we shall, in time, find a cure for AIDS.'

'But before that, hundreds will die!' Kathy said, passionately. 'And it still doesn't excuse it. Don't you care?' They stopped by the wall of the hotel under a street lamp. 'That isn't love!'

'Of course I care,' he said, angrily. 'Love should be sweet and kind and as deep as the sea, but only a few are lucky enough to discover it.' He raised her face between his hands and looked deeply into her eyes, where tears threatened, making dark blue pools of light.

He kissed her gently and her lips wanted to cling in an unfamiliar sweetness, as if she had glimpsed a rose garden through a half open door. He put her from him slowly, and the roses faded.

Lisa Cooper was brought up on the Isle of Wight and went to a well-known London teaching hospital to train as a nurse. After a short spell as theatre sister, she married an accountant, and their two children also have medical connections, her son being a biologist with a pharmaceutical firm and her daughter a medical scientist in a famous hospital for sick children.

Lisa Cooper feels it is important to show the complete professional integrity of the hero and heroine as well as their deep felt emotions, and she makes a point of carefully researching latest developments in surgery and medical science. Writing as a second career began at home when she was unable to go back to nursing in hospital, and she has now written over thirty books.

Previous Titles

LOVE'S HEALING TOUCH
THE RIGHT TO LIFE

AMSTERDAM ENCOUNTER

BY

LISA COOPER

MILLS & BOON LIMITED
ETON HOUSE   18-24 PARADISE ROAD
RICHMOND   SURREY   TW9 1SR

First published in Great Britain 1989 by Mills & Boon Limited

© Lisa Cooper 1989

Australian copyright 1989 Philippine copyright 1989 This edition 1989

ISBN 0 263 76531 8

Set in Palacio 10 on 11 pt. 03 – 8909 – 51499

Typeset in Great Britain by JCL Graphics, Bristol

Made and Printed in Great Britain

CHAPTER ONE

'BUT this isn't my case!' Kathy heard her own voice and it sounded hollow, as if a sudden bubble of silence surrounded her, and the faces of the other passengers faded as they drew back from what might be trouble. There was a kind of relief in their faces, as if they knew that they were safe and that whatever touched this pretty auburn-haired girl could not concern them.

'You carried this piece of luggage on your trolley and showed no sign of it being strange when we asked you to open it,' the man said coldly, and Kathy wondered how her aunt had ever managed to give her the impression that the Dutch were a warm and sympathetic race.

Her mouth was dry and she stumbled over her words, knowing that this did nothing to help her, but being powerless to hide her panic. 'It belongs to a man who has gone on with his secretary,' she began, and then saw the slightly tired cynicism in the eyes of the big Customs officer.

'Would you step over here, Madam?' he said.

Kathy cast a despairing look towards the exit where two minutes earlier her patient and his secretary had walked away to wait for her in the car that they had been told would call for them at the airport, at Schiphol, fifteen kilometres away from the outskirts of Amsterdam. She picked up her handbag and followed the silent man and the boy who had appeared to push the heavily laden trolley.

In the small, bare room, the Customs officer laid out the smart leather case that had surfaced as he'd made his first perfunctory examination of her luggage. 'I can explain that,' she began.

'Please do,' he said. 'You do know this case?' She nodded. He opened the bright hasps and the two sides fell apart to reveal syringes and capsules and an elastic band that could be used to compress the upper arm when an intravenous injection was given. 'You know this case?' he repeated more harshly. 'What drug are you on?'

She stared at him. This couldn't be true! An hour ago she had been sitting in the first-class comfort of a jet aircraft, looking forward to what promised to be a very interesting visit to a city of which she had been told by her partly Dutch aunt, the dear soul who had cared for her and her father ever since Kathy was a baby.

Her patient, Sir Elliot Russell, had a heart condition that had responded completely to major surgery, and he now needed treatment only for his asthma, which had been much better since his convalescence and in Kathy's opinion had its roots in the stress caused by his previous illness. It just couldn't be true! This man suspected her of bringing drugs for her own use into the country, when all that the phials contained were ephedrine, adrenalin and other stronger preparations for asthma, none of which Sir Elliot might have to use now, but which had been ordered by his own doctor, in case of a relapse or any attack brought on by sudden shock or stress.

'Look at the labels,' she said with more confidence. 'I am a nursing sister, and I came with Sir Elliot Russell from London to look after him after heart surgery. There are stimulants there, and medication for asthma, and that is all.' She looked at the officer more defiantly. 'He will wonder where I am and be worried, and that is the last thing his doctor wants to happen just now.'

The man looked less hostile. He picked up one of the syringes and tore open the sterile cover, sniffed at it and put it down on the other two that he had opened when he had first seen them. 'They seem not to have been used,' he said.

'They were sterile until you contaminated them,' said Kathy. 'Now I shall have to obtain new ones, or have these re-sterilised! I can't use them on my patient in that condition.'

'I'm sorry, *mevrouw*, but I have to do my duty.' He handed one of the phials to the boy and spoke rapidly in Dutch. 'Wait here until we know what this contains,' he commanded, and Kathy sank on to the hard plastic chair he indicated. She thought more clearly now that she was alone, and asked the woman who stood impassively by the door if she could send a message to Sir Elliot, but the woman either did not understand or had no intention of answering, as she gave no indication of having heard the request. Kathy untied her scarf in the stuffy atmosphere of the closed room that smelled of tobacco smoke and dust, and thrust the silk square into her capacious handbag. Her fingers touched a stiff envelope and she took it out eagerly. Of course! The letter!

She rose from the chair and waved the letter under the unresponsive nose of the woman officer. 'Take this to the officer-in-charge,' she said clearly. How could she have forgotten that she had been given all the details of Sir Elliot's medication and possible treatment in a concisely written document signed by his own physician? When Rebecca Wilson, Sir Elliot's secretary, had given it to her under the watchful eye of her employer, she had put it safely in her bag and almost forgotten it, thinking that she would have it ready for reference, but sensing no urgency to memorise the contents, as she knew exactly what to do if an emergency arose now that she had all the drugs that could be used.

The swing door opened and the officer returned. The woman gave him the envelope and he opened it carefully, with the reluctance of one who was uncertain if he could read a letter written in a foreign language, however well he spoke English. His expression cleared. 'The doctor had the sense to write both in English and Dutch, Madam. If you had shown this to me earlier, you could have saved yourself much embarrassment,' he added sternly.

'I was hardly expecting to be accused of drug-taking,' she said. 'You didn't give me time to think clearly!'

He smiled for the first time. 'That is our policy. The greater the shock at first, the better the result for us, and the sooner a confession.'

'And if I had not convinced you?' she asked.

'A body search and many, many questions,' he said smoothly.

Kathy sat down heavily. 'I wish I had never come to your horrible country,' she whispered. 'From what I hear, you have a bigger drug problem than most countries, and one that you allow to exist, and yet you looked on me as a potential criminal.'

'We have troubles enough of our own, and hope to keep out any more,' he said. 'Do not believe all the Press say, *mevrouw*. We are a practical country. We face what is here and try to erase it, but we do not

ignore what people think they need, and we try to
find a way that injures only a few while channelling
the more depraved needs of men and women into
certain areas of the city. Believe that we do not
encourage drugs and, when you return, declare such
things as syringes and medicines.'

He went towards the door. 'May I go?' Kathy
asked.

'Of course. The boy will wheel the trolley to the car.
We have told Sir Elliot that you were delayed by a
case that refused to shut.' He grinned. 'Enjoy your
stay in Holland, *mevrouw.*'

'I am here on duty, not from choice,' she said
coldly. 'I doubt if I shall bother to explore
Amsterdam, and the sooner I get back to London, the
better!'

He glanced at the envelope in her hand. 'Don't lose
that. Someone, and a Dutchman, by his first name,
cared enough to make sure that you could travel
freely while carrying very suspicious baggage. You
see, we are a considerate people, and we prefer to
help rather than to condemn.'

He had gone before Kathy could reply, and she
meekly followed the boy out into the sunshine,
wondering if she would ever forget that little room
and the dull expression on the face of the woman
who might have had to search her body in ways that
made her shudder to consider.

'What kept you?' asked Rebecca. Sir Elliot Russell
sighed and watched the luggage being loaded into a
second car. 'He's getting impatient,' the secretary
said in a low voice. 'Can't stand women who keep
him waiting,' she added with satisfaction, and Kathy
realised for the first time that Rebecca, who had been
so helpful before they left England, resented her in

some way.

'A slight hitch,' said Kathy, and smiled. 'The Customs here are very thorough, and no one told me that they would query the sterile packs.' She spoke clearly, seeing no reason to hide anything, and Sir Elliot looked at her in surprise.

'But Becky wrote to them before we left and explained that I wanted to leave the airport quickly, and that we would be bringing a nursing sister and certain drugs with us.'

'They can't have received it in time,' said Rebecca hastily, and Kathy wondered, for a fleeting moment, if the letter had ever been sent.

'That is absurd!' Sir Elliot said peevishly. 'You must write again in the strongest terms, Becky, and I will sign the letter before it goes. I could have been waiting here for hours.' He glanced at Kathy, and his usual benevolent expression returned. 'I knew that you would not keep me waiting. That is one of the things that impressed me when we met. You were punctual on duty at the hospital and when I made an interview to ask you to come with us here, and you were ready well before the time we had to leave for the airport, while Becky was still fussing over my papers.'

'I had to get them in order as we shall be away for a while,' said Rebecca. 'You know you would be upset if I hadn't brought everything but the kitchen sink!' She spoke with the familiarity of someone who was fond of her employer and knew his ways.

'I think you did bring the kitchen sink,' he said, but now he was teasing. 'If we had any more baggage, we'd need yet another car.'

'The Customs were right to check,' said Kathy, reluctant to show any resentment of her treatment and anxious that the incident should not blow up into a major row. Now that they were driving away from the airport, it was more like a bad dream, and receded as the car took them swiftly to the luxury hotel where they were booked into a suite of rooms on the top floor. 'I showed them the letter from Dr Raynor,' she said. 'He must be a man of some influence, as they took one look and let me go.'

'Michiel is very meticulous and cares about his patients,' said Sir Elliot. 'Very well-qualified, and a man I'd choose to have with me in a tight spot.' Kathy smiled. Sir Elliot sounded as if he might be ready to tell her about one of the campaigns in which he had fought in World War Two when he was a very young army officer. That dates your Dr Michiel Raynor, she thought. Dear old pals from way back who had suffered together, drunk together, and probably chased the same women.

The car slowed down and the driver paused to let a flow of cyclists pass on to the narrow lane of a canal-bank. More followed, and it took several minutes to negotiate the way to the hotel on the side of the Amstel. In spite of her earlier resentment and discomfort, Kathy took a deep breath and gazed at the stretch of blue water. The tall, slender trees lining the canals were softly green, and blurred the outlines of the tall, narrow houses that flanked the water. After the grey bustle of the centre of Amsterdam, this was peace and elegance, and yet had a kind of homeliness that was endearing.

'One of the oldest of the waterways,' said Sir Elliot with satisfaction. 'I hope to do a lot of work here, so you can help me,' he said firmly.

'Sir Elliot writes about the sixteenth and seventeenth centuries,' said Rebecca. 'And we came

here to research, as well as for rest.' Her mouth
curved in a slightly malicious smile. 'I don't think he
needs a nurse at all, and if you hate history you're in
for a very boring stay.'

'Sister Tyler and I had a very long chat during our
first meeting in hospital, when you were sending off
the telexes,' said Sir Elliot. He grinned as if he liked
to have some secrets about which his secretary knew
nothing. 'She told me of her father and his interests
in Dutch culture, and about her aunt who cared for
them as housekeeper. She had Dutch connections,
and so has Sister Tyler.' He looked disapproving. 'I
do need a nurse, if only to give me the confidence to
do what I need to do here. I know that Sister Tyler
can cope with any emergency. Michiel checked with
her training school and said that the Princess Beatrice
Hospital in London is one of the finest in the world,
and they turn out some terrific nurses. So even if I
need no more than an aspirin for a headache, I do
need a well-qualified and attractive woman to be with
me at all times, to give me confidence.'

'I did warn you that I might hear from VSO at any
time, Sir Elliot,' said Kathy. She smiled. 'I am only
free to be here until they decide when I can leave for
India. I really feel that you have no need of a nurse
now. Rebecca has looked after you a lot and knows
what you need, so why me?'

'Michiel was adamant. He said I must take a nurse
with me if I intended working, as nobody knows how
much stress I can take with my other condition. He
saw your references and thinks he has met you. In
any case, he chose you and you should be flattered.
He doesn't suffer fools, and he is a very dear friend of
mine. I thought he might favour a sister from his own
training school, but obviously he thinks very highly

of the Princess Beatrice Hospital.' Sir Elliot looked at her curiously. 'Are you sure that you two don't know each other?'

Kathy tried to remember a doctor of about fifty or sixty who had visited her training school. She shrugged. So many men and women came to Beattie's to watch surgical procedures that were pioneered there, or to observe the wonders of medical science and orthopaedic advances that made the hospital famous all over the world, that it was impossible to recall one man, who might have spoken to her once or perhaps had heard her name when she was working in the operating-theatre.

'I can't remember the name at all,' she said. 'But he certainly made sure that anyone reading his letter would be in no doubt about your condition, and that you might have a need of the drugs we brought with us.'

'He's a fine man, and very gifted,' said Sir Elliot. 'Becky is very fond of him, and most of his colleagues admire him, even when he rides his hobby-horse and gets all hot under the collar about drug abuse.'

'Is he in general practice or does he just take a few private patients?' asked Kathy, visualising a man half-retired, with his own set life-style.

'He's a very busy man,' said Sir Elliot, and picked up his English newspapers and some letters that he had not as yet read, but which Becky had brought from the post that had arrived just before they had left for Amsterdam. His manner showed that he wanted to be left in peace to read them. Kathy smiled. Sir Elliot's idea of a busy schedule might not be hers, but Dr Raynor must be quite nice if he had helped her, however unwittingly, out of what could have been a very horrific situation.

'Sister?' She hurried into the main bedroom where Sir Elliot handed her a paper that had been included in a letter addressed to him. It was lightly sealed with her name on the cover. 'Further instructions, no doubt,' he said drily. 'If he tells you that wine is forbidden, forget it. You are here to look after me, which means you spoil me and give in to my every whim!' He laughed. 'Don't look so anxious. Open it. It won't bite you.'

'Dear Sister Tyler,' she read. 'By now, you will be well on your way to the hotel. Make sure that he rests at once. I suggest a dry sherry before dinner, and an early night with no piles of books ready for him to read during the night. You have sedatives to use if necessary, and don't be fooled by his air of calm. He's a neurotic, and has all kinds of hidden fears that could lead to an asthma attack, however well he appears. I know the old boy well, and I shall be over to see him soon. Any problems, ring this number. I have a friend in Amsterdam, a Dr Johannes Wittener, in whom I have confidence. He speaks good English and knows about local clinics and hospitals.'

She looked up, but Sir Elliot was lying on the bed, reading his mail, and seemed to have forgotten her. She folded the letter and put it in her handbag. Was Dr Michiel Raynor a fussy old man who had just one of two prize patients, or was he younger, more in touch with current medicine, and with a clearer picture than she could have of her patient?

'Do you want to go out?' Rebecca's voice broke into her thoughts. 'You can go. I'll be here if he needs anything.' She sounded friendly, and spoke carelessly as if there was nothing to worry her, but Kathy had the impression that she wanted her out of the way.

'I'll unpack and get settled in,' said Kathy with a smile. 'We haven't arranged a schedule yet, and I think I'd better be here until Sir Elliot decides when I am to have time off.'

'There's no need,' said Rebecca. 'I arrange all his schedules, and I can tell him that I gave you permission to go.'

'I have to sort out the pack that the Customs opened,' said Kathy. 'It's as well that he needs no injections. There is only one sterile syringe now, and I must sterilise the others before we need them—if indeed we do need the more potent drugs at all. He seems so well that I can't see it being necessary to give him heavy medication, and he has simple inhalers to use if he feels wheezy.' She saw no need to say what was in the note from Dr Raynor. 'But I must have everything ready to cover every contingency. I am not here as a tourist or a guest. I feel guilty as it is, accepting a good fee for doing hardly anything but giving up my time to him.'

'You sound as bad as Dr Raynor,' said Rebecca. She flounced away, clearly annoyed, and when Sir Elliot called for Sister Tyler after only an hour, demanding that she take his pulse and blood pressure as he could hear his own heart beating fast, Kathy knew that she had been wise to stay in the hotel.

'It's fine,' she said with a gentle smile, when at last she put away the sphygmomanometer and her stethoscope. 'It's been a trying day, and you need a good sleep tonight, but I suspect you are hungry. The snack on the plane was at the wrong time to enjoy it, and I noticed that you hardly touched yours.' She glanced at her watch. 'Why not rest for another hour, then shower and take an early dinner? I'll send for a glass of sherry or white wine, and you can enjoy it here in your room before you go down.'

He smiled. 'I might have known that Michiel would send me an angel.' He slid back against the pillows and Kathy covered him with a light blanket. 'Call me with a large dry sherry and I'll take it with me to the bathroom. Order what you like, and of course for Becky, but she knows the drill and has probably ordered fruit and wine enough to last a week.'

'He's fine,' Kathy said when Rebecca raised her eyebrows as if to ask. 'I can understand him being apprehensive after all he's been through, and I think a normal life is what he needs. Do you order the sherry, or would you like me to do it? A small drink is often better than a tranquilliser in the evening.'

'I've ordered some, and we have a fridge in the sitting-room filled with different drinks, so help yourself and they will add it to the bill. We shall need lots of spa water, and spring water for his whisky, and for Dr Raynor when he comes here.' Rebecca blushed. 'What did you mean by normal life? Does that include sex?'

'I suppose so.' Kathy looked thoughtful. 'I'm not the one to ask. Why not mention it to his dear old friend? I suppose men of his age still need love in all its aspects if they are that way inclined, and as for his health, there is no reason for abstinence now that he is fit.'

'He likes pretty women and we were . . . close before he had his op. Not that anything happened,' Rebecca added quickly, 'but I thought that one day we could be even closer. I'm very fond of him and he has come to depend on me.' Her mouth quivered, and Kathy realised that her arrival must have been a shock to the woman who had worked for Sir Elliot for some years.

'He is very distinguished,' said Kathy. She laughed. 'I'm right off men of all ages just now, and I haven't had a lot of luck in my choice of lover so far, so perhaps if I team up with his geriatric friend we can make a foursome!'

'Funny girl!' Rebecca gave Kathy a look that held curiosity and sly humour. 'Put on your beige cardy and slippers, dear. The geriatric friend is on his way and will be with us for dinner.'

'Good! I want to thank him for that letter. I could have been in a real spot without it, and after seeing the woman who sat in with me, waiting for the phial to be identified, I am more and more grateful each time I think of it.'

'I'm sorry about that,' said Rebecca impulsively. 'I was a cow! I didn't send the letter, and I thought that they would catch you. I really hoped you'd burst into tears and go home, but now I hate myself, and hope you'll stay. At least we can take it in turns to be here and cover each other's off-duty.'

'So now you know I'm not a threat to you, I can forget what happened? I ought to be really angry, but life's too short! Just remember, you owe me a big favour, and one day I might claim it,' Kathy added lightly.

Kathy changed into a slim sheath of fine cotton that made her dark blue eyes seem even more deep, and highlighted the sheen in her hair. The mixture of pale greens and yellows in the fabric was cool and restrained, so that she knew that she could appear in the smart restaurant, but wouldn't look conspicuous.

'No beige cardy?' asked the older woman, who had appeared in a soft blue sweater and skirt, and wore ridiculously high-heeled sandals of twisted pastel leather straps.

'Nothing to raise the blood pressure,' Kathy assured her, and felt a sudden warmth towards the plump blonde who so obviously looked on Sir Elliot as her private property. 'I have to pack the syringes that were unsterilised, as the porter knows of a clinic that will do them for me. I explained that they were for an asthmatic, to save him thinking the worst! I couldn't bear anyone else to think I'm a mainliner!'

'He could get you new disposables easily,' said Rebecca. 'They can get anything. Hall porters bring in special drinks, drugs sometimes, they book theatres, and they certainly smuggle women into the hotels as and when needed.' She saw that Kathy was shocked. 'Not all of them, silly, but in a place like this you can be sure they are asked for everything you can imagine, and some things you can't!'

'I'll help Sir Elliot to dress and ask him if he'd like the menu before we go down to eat,' suggested Kathy. 'Just give me ten minutes first to get the pack done.'

She closed the bedroom door slightly, as it opened on to the sitting-room of the suite and she felt that her unpacked luggage made the room untidy, but she didn't close the door completely in case she was called. She laid the syringes out on the bed. She knew that she could buy disposables, but that would have to wait until she found a chemist who sold them with a full warranty that they were sterile. So much had been said and written about infection from dirty needles and syringes that she could afford to take no chances, and preferred to use the ones she had brought with her. She held one up to the light and frowned. The officer had been rough with it and it was cracked, so she wrapped it in tissues and put it on the bed, ready to dispose of it in a waste basket.

There was one still in its sterile pack. Would that be enough until she could buy more? Surely it was unlikely that her patient would need more than one injection before tomorrow, even if he needed that? The rubber band to compress the arm seemed fine, but she resolved to buy another as it was beginning to fray and it might be quite old.

She pulled it to test its elasticity, and then gasped as it flew from her hand and shot across the room under the dressing-table. 'Damn!' she said softly. She bent down, but couldn't reach the band from that position. More laddered tights! she thought, and, with an air of resignation, kicked off her high-heeled court shoes and went down on her knees to peer under the furniture.

It was further back than she could reach until she was almost flat on the floor, and when at last she touched it and hooked it onto one finger to draw it out, she was flushed and slightly breathless. 'Got you,' she said with relief, and relaxed on the floor, her arm extended holding the broad rubber band, and her hair dishevelled.

She raised her head and began to get up, then stared at a pair of well-polished, very solid and respectable English brogues. Her gaze went upwards over immaculate worsted trousers that sat well over taut thighs, to a white and grey striped shirt, and a slightly surreal necktie of dazzling brilliance that was in direct contrast to the rest of the sober attire.

She forgot the tie. The face above it was angry, and the anger was directed at her, although he was not looking at her, but staring at the syringes and phials on the bed. Kathy sat up and brushed dust from her shirt. 'Hello,' she said. 'Who are you? I could have done with a long arm a minute ago.'

He picked up the broken syringe and held it to the light.

'It does help to have an extra hand to hold that band,' he said icily. 'Now suppose you tell me what you are doing in a private apartment, taking a fix as if you belong here? I came here expecting to find a nursing sister and find a . . . junkie. Why don't you just get out of here before I have you busted?'

Kathy stared. 'Not again!' she whispered. Did all men in Amsterdam think she took drugs?

'Again? You mean you've been busted in all the best hotels?' His voice was cold and he turned slowly to face her, as she swept her hair from her eyes in a gesture of defiance. His expression changed to one of surprise and horror. 'I just don't believe it,' he said slowly.

Kathy stood and brushed down the front of her dress. She slipped into her shoes and felt less vulnerable now that she had no need to look up so far into the dark brown eyes. She glanced towards the bed. The open medical-case lay there, with the phials in a neat row after she had checked them. She had been about to put them away before she had had to grovel on the floor after the rubber band. He held the cracked syringe, in its wrapping of tissue, as if it had been discarded after use, and the whole room was not as neat as she would have liked. She sensed that the man was watching her closely, and realised that he was waiting for her to react to whatever it was that he thought she had injected into her arm. But there was something more in his eyes. Pain as if he had suffered a shock, and anger that had no roots in righteous indignation, but held an edge of despair.

Once more she pushed back the heavy swathe of hair from her eyes, and he reached over and gripped her arm.

'Leave me alone! You're hurting me!' she cried. 'Who are you? This is my room, and I'll thank you to get the hell out of here at once!' The sudden grip on her arm was cruel, as if he wanted to hurt her, and yet she felt as if he might easily have used this force to take her close and kiss her.

He turned her arm to inspect the soft underside of her forearm, then let it fall, looking puzzled. He grabbed her other hand and did the same, but saw only the unblemished skin with the slight early summer tan making it smooth and warm and delectable.

With an expression of growing embarrassment, he looked at the phials on the bed and picked up one to read the words inscribed on the glass. 'Salbutamol!' He picked up another. 'Hydrocortisone!' he said. 'These are for acute asthma.'

'My patient has that condition and, like the well-trained nursing sister that I am, I check equipment whenever I arrive in a strange place, and have everything ready for use, however unlikely it is that it will be needed!' Kathy began to pack the phials away carefully, but with trembling hands. 'I don't know who you are, but please leave before I call for the house detective. That is, if they have anyone here who is likely to protect guests from insulting behaviour. I doubt it, somehow, and if anyone else accuses me of taking drugs in this horrible one-track-minded city, I shall scream!'

'I apologise,' he said in a flat voice. 'It was a natural mistake. If you will lie on the floor with your skirt up to your thighs and your hair over your face, with a tourniquet in your hand and a used syringe on the bed, what *are* people to think?' He put up his hands in a defensive gesture as she looked even more annoyed. 'OK! OK. I know it's cracked. I checked, but a situation where a girl is showing a lot of very nice leg, lying on the floor without shoes and with her hair in a mess, in that scene, it points one of two ways, doesn't it?'

'Two ways?' she asked automatically.

He grinned. 'Amsterdam has other things on her mind than drugs. There are other vices that can be bought quite readily. No more than other cities, but in a way I think they are dealt with more honestly, and not hidden away as if the problem doesn't exist.'

Kathy tried to ignore him, and was aware that she needed a hair brush and a fresh application of lipstick before she could appear before Sir Elliot. 'I don't know you, and I can't think why you are here. Please go away.'

'I am visiting Sir Elliot Russell,' he said. 'I was sent to say hello to you, Sister Tyler, and I apologise for not . . . seeing you for who you are.' He grinned. 'As for leaving, I shall go when I'm ready.'

'Who are you?' Kathy swung round to face him, consternation growing fast. He knew about the drugs, and he was obviously not ill at ease in the suite, so he must have been invited. Dr Raynor had mentioned a Dutch doctor in the letter, but this man looked very British to her untutored eyes. She recalled the officer at the airport. Without his accent, he could have been British, with fairish hair and blue eyes, but this man looked more Celtic, with dark hair and eyes and a firm cleft chin.

'I know who you are,' he said. 'Let me introduce myself. Michiel Raynor. Welcome to Amsterdam.'

He laughed, and humour mixed with a great relief lit the sombre depths of his eyes. 'I believe we are all having dinner together.' He turned at the door. 'That is, if you tidy your hair and wipe that smudge off your cheek, and promise to wear shoes.'

Kathy put a hand to one cheek, then went to close the door after him.

'It's the other one,' he said mildly.

'Why don't you take off that terrible tie?' she said sweetly. 'My patient has to beware of shocks.' She closed the door and bolted it, then slowly brushed her hair and retouched her make-up, wondering why her eyes shone and her hands trembled, as if she had emerged from a dream and not a nightmare. She tried to recall if she had met him or seen him somewhere, light-years ago, but dismissed the idea. She could not possibly have forgotten him.

CHAPTER TWO

'HOW do you like our geriatric friend?' whispered Rebecca as she passed over a basket of bread-sticks to Kathy.

'I can see that I must believe about a quarter of what you tell me,' said Kathy. 'And as to the man in question, I have not made up my mind.' She ignored the gleeful expression and helped herself to butter. Becky! she thought. How can a woman of at least thirty-five call herself that, as if she were a fluffy, kittenish seventeen-year-old, all boobs and no brain? But if her real name was Rebecca, that was even worse, as her very blonde hair and heavily made-up eyes didn't match the dignity of that ancient and beautiful name. Kathy sighed. In my next life, I'd like to be a helpless-looking blonde, and all the men will treat me as a delicate piece of Dresden china! she thought. Her natural humour made her giggle as she glanced at the serious face of Dr Michiel Raynor. That was one man who wouldn't fall for fluttering eyelashes.

Rebecca glanced towards the two men who were deep in conversation on the other side of the table for four, and whose voices were muted under the soft, insistent music from the stereo. 'I didn't say anything about him,' she protested. 'It was you who jumped to the conclusion that he must be older than he is.'

'So long as he's a good doctor and cares for Sir Elliot well, that is all that matters,' said Kathy.

'He came into your room, didn't he? I sent him there to meet you. Thought it might be a nice surprise,' Rebecca went on. 'Not that he's very interested in women, as far as I know, but it would be useful if you could do all the social bits with him when Sir Elliot and I are entertaining,' she suggested with an air of condescension, and a cautious glance at Kathy's face.

'Don't worry,' said Kathy. 'I shall fit in with whatever Sir Elliot wants me to do while I'm here, even if it means sitting opposite that terrible tie.' She gave a look of mock surprise. 'Surely you don't think I have designs on your dear old employer? All I want is peace and quiet before I go to work in the Third World.'

Rebecca wrinkled her nose. 'I couldn't do anything like that,' she said. 'All that dirt and disease and those starving people.' She took another bread-stick and then put it back into the tall cut-glass container. 'A bit of starvation might be good for me,' she said regretfully. 'I can't look at a bread roll or a baked potato without it going straight to my hips.'

'My aunt used to put a notice above the fridge door, saying "A moment on the lips and a lifetime on the hips."' Kathy laughed. 'She ignored it herself, but trotted out the saying whenever she had friends to tea who were overweight. Then she'd try to make me eat so much that I'd end up as plump as she was.'

'She didn't make a good job of that,' said Rebecca resentfully, eyeing the slim girl at her side. 'Life is very unfair.' She spoke in a louder voice, and Dr Raynor looked across at her with a quizzical smile.

'You sound a little less than happy, Becky,' he said. 'Why is life unfair?' Kathy stared. He was smiling as if indulging a child. She stifled a smile. Or a patient who was a bit dim and needed a soft approach.

'You'd better ask Kathy. She was the one who was busted for carrying drug-taking equipment into the country.' The memory of Kathy's discomfiture seemed to give her renewed pleasure, and it was obvious to Kathy that she must be careful of her trust in anything that she said or did in the future. Rebecca's abject apology had been convincing, but now she had the same old malicious little smile on her lips—the smile of a troublemaker. Kathy lowered her gaze and snapped the bread-stick sharply.

'Poor Sister Tyler. You've had quite an introduction to Amsterdam,' the pleasant voice said, but Kathy suspected that he, too, was laughing at her. She felt excluded, as if they were all laughing at her—even Sir Elliot, who sensed that there was a hidden joke and smiled approval. Dr Raynor called the patient Elliot and was on easy terms with Becky, but the two men called her Sister Tyler, and now they had her humiliation to enjoy. She glanced up and was surprised to that the dark brown eyes were not laughing, but held a kind of gentle chiding. 'You mustn't judge Holland by one unfortunate encounter,' he said. 'While you are here, we must make sure that you see some of the places of interest. There are canal trips and coach tours to other parts of Holland that could be fascinating if you enjoy history and seeing different places.' He thought for a moment. 'As a nursing sister, you might like to visit one of the fine modern hospitals here.'

Kathy nodded politely, but felt oddly disappointed. He made her sound as if she was a spinster of uncertain age who had to be entertained, and might be persuaded to go alone to places that he had no intention of seeing nor desire to visit. Rebecca was smiling, safe in the knowledge that neither of the men showed any sign of making any effort to fill the off-duty of the interloper whom she had dreaded coming to Holland. 'We can all go on the canals,' she suggested with a burst of generosity. 'I like cruising along on the boats that serve dinner on board. Sister Tyler shouldn't walk about the city alone at night.'

'I walk about London and Bristol at night,' said Kathy. 'I've never had any trouble. I am here on duty, and there is no need to plan my off-duty for me. I can collect leaflets, and with the help of a phrase-book I can get along anywhere.' She felt her colour rising and lifted her chin defiantly.

'And not run into trouble?' Dr Raynor laughed and his dark eyes mocked her as if she needed a nursemaid or a bodyguard. 'When are you letting Sister Tyler out of your sight for a few hours, Elliot? Someone ought to see that she doesn't fall into a canal, or get lost in the back-streets.'

Kathy didn't know if she wanted his help or not. The dark eyes were now teasing as if she were a child or, heaven forbid, a simpering woman like Rebecca to be jollied along, but at least he was now friendly and didn't glower at her as he had done in the bedroom.

'I shall visit the Rijksmuseum tomorrow,' announced Sir Elliot. 'Just a gentle introduction to research,' he insisted. 'Nothing strenuous, but a very self-indulgent wallow in Rembrandt and Hals and, if I have time, a quick look at the gable-stones on the roofs of the houses in Graven Straat.' He smiled at his secretary, who was looking glum. 'You must learn to enjoy it, my dear. I hope to do a lot of museums in the future, but you can wander while I sit and look at the *Night Watch*, and Sister Tyler can stay with me.'

'Is the Vermeer collection there, too?' asked Kathy. Her eyes sparkled. 'It would be wonderful to see the original of *Young Woman Reading a Letter* and some of his smaller paintings.'

Dr Raynor watched her as she asked other questions, and Kathy forgot that she hated Holland, and remembered only the plans she had made when her father was alive that had never come to fruition as he became weaker and could no longer travel.

'And in the afternoon, you rest,' said Dr Raynor firmly. 'Becky can see to your papers and I shall take Sister Tyler walking by the canals, guidebook in hand and very stout shoes on her feet—that is, if she has anything suitable.'

Kathy blushed. Sir Elliot had said quite firmly that he wished her to dress as she would on holiday, and he didn't want to see another nurse's uniform for as long as he lived, so the shoes she now wore were slender and of fine leather, marvellously comfortable and well-made, but not exactly duty shoes. Was the doctor hinting that she should dress more formally? She lifted her chin and looked at him. It hadn't stopped him from eyeing her legs as she had lain on the floor of the bedroom, and she had felt his swift and very penetrating appraisal as she came into the dining-room. 'I have some trainers with me,' she said. 'Even I have heard about the cobbled side-streets here.'

'Well, you can wear them with Michiel, but I prefer my women to dress smartly,' said Sir Elliot. 'You look very nice, my dear, and I love to see a woman in high heels.' Kathy repressed a smile. So that was why Becky teetered along on those heels! He laughed. 'Trainers and jeans might be more in keeping with Michiel's tie. I am intrigued. He refuses to tell me where he got it, and I have never seen anything quite like it.'

'It's very cheerful,' said Kathy demurely, but a hint of mischief showed in the dimple at the side of her mouth. 'Perhaps a gift that he has to wear to please the giver. I remember a ghastly sweater that a dear relative made for me that I had to wear just once when I went to see her, and felt self-conscious all the way to the house as it was too hot to wear a jacket to hide the awful stripes.'

Sir Elliot laughed, but when she glanced at Michiel Raynor he was scowling. Oh dear, he really likes it, she thought.

'What happened to the sweater?' asked Becky.

'I gave it to a girl who was so dark and lovely that the colours glowed on her and she adored it,' said Kathy. 'I almost wished I'd kept it when I saw her wearing it, but I knew it wasn't really for me.'

'I am very fond of this tie, and I will have no one insulting it,' said Dr Raynor, with a protective smoothing of the silk monstrosity.

'I know! It was given by a rich patient who has promised to leave you all her money,' suggested Rebecca.

'Why a gift from a woman?' asked Sir Elliot, who was enjoying the exchange. 'Why do you think he didn't buy it?'

'Only a woman would g ve a man a tie like that and dare him to wear it to show that he cared,' Rebecca said shrewdly.

Dr Raynor's face took on a rich redness that had nothing to do with the wine or the warmth of the restaurant. He helped himself to more asparagus and said nothing, but Kathy knew that Rebecca had touched a sore spot in the doctor's defences. A woman had given him the tie, and in her mind Kathy could see slender and sensual fingers adjusting it for him in a way that said, This man is mine.

'More asparagus?' asked Rebecca. 'I'll finish it if you've all had enough.'

The meal progressed, and when Sir Elliot began to drink his specially made decaffeinated coffee Kathy slipped away to make sure that his room was ready for him to go to bed. She tidied the pile of magazines that had fallen on the floor, and paused to admire the book containing beautiful prints of some of the Old Masters that she hoped to see the next day. The flowers that Rebecca had arranged in the bedroom looked fresh and were arranged with care, but Kathy frowned. She had not known Sir Elliot long enough to have his full medical history. Her brief had been to nurse him after his bypass operation and then, when he had asked if she could stay with him for a while, she had been told that he had a history of asthmatic attacks—none of which had occurred during his stay in the private wing of Beattie's.

Flowers in the bedroom of an asthmatic seemed all wrong. Kathy knew that asthma was caused by a variety of foreign substances that triggered attacks, ranging from dog hair and cat fur to the pollen from grasses and some flowers. Food could have a bearing on the attacks, but his notes showed nothing of this. Or did they? Rather guiltily she went to her own room and opened the envelope that she had not had time to read, as it had arrived from the registrar at Beattie's just before they had left for Amsterdam, and Sir Elliot had kept her talking on the plane to hide his own fear of flying.

She glanced down the page, taking in facts that she

knew about his heart operation, and then saw a note at the bottom, brief and seemingly unimportant. 'Sir Elliot has a history of asthma, probably psychological in origin as there have been no attacks while under our care, but due to his being nursed in a dust-free environment with no flowers or other extraneous matter within contact we might have a too simple picture, and I suggest the following drugs should be at hand for emergencies while in a foreign country.' The list of drugs followed, and matched the contents of the bag that had caused her so much embarrassment. The note was signed by the senior registrar in charge of his case at the Princess Beatrice Hospital in London.

'So, even if we don't know what allergies you might have, no flowers in your room,' Kathy said, and went back to remove them. The flower vase was overfull of water, and some spilled as she lifted it. She put it down on a tray that held a bottle of spa water and one of pure lemon juice, and reached for a tissue to mop up the small puddle. She tossed the wet tissue into the waste bin and turned to pick up the flowers.

'For crying out loud! Don't you know anything about asthmatics?' She stood with the vase in her hands, her face framed in the sweet-scented carnations and freesias. Dr Raynor took the vase and walked into the sitting-room with it, leaving a trail of spilled water as he went. 'He's on his way up. Open that window and let some air in here.'

'I wasn't putting flowers in his room, I was removing them,' said Kathy. 'I read his notes and they said he hadn't had an attack while in hospital, but flowers did seem a bad idea.' She was flushed and annoyed. Each time this man appeared she felt at a disadvantage, and he did nothing to lessen the feeling.

'Well, whatever is the truth, get these into your room for the night and make sure they stay by the sitting-room window tomorrow if he insists on flowers.'

Kathy forced the window open with difficulty, and the evening air came in from over the Amstel, fresh and sweet and smelling of the sea. 'It's a warm night, so we can leave the window open and turn off the air-conditioning,' she said.

'You didn't arrange those flowers?' he asked. She shook her head. 'Surely Becky wouldn't have left them here?'

'She said that Sir Elliot loves flowers and likes her to buy them whenever they are away from home, but she should know that they aren't a good idea in the bedroom.' Kathy watched the curtains move softly in the fresh air. 'If he was a bad case, he would have been tested for allergies. I know very little about him before his heart bypass op, and even this letter from the registrar gives me no details of his other case history.'

'I thought my letter was quite explicit,' Dr Raynor said, the expression of disapproval returning. 'Don't you read notes and instructions? You saw that I spelled out that he was allergic to carnations and cat fur, and mildly allergic to rye-grass pollen. I did the tests myself.'

'What letter? I had this one from the registrar in the private patient wing at Beattie's, and the one that you sent listing the drugs that were being brought into Holland, but you made no reference to his allergies,' Kathy said firmly.

'I sent another, addressed to the sister-in-charge as I wasn't completely sure who would be with him, and it was of no interest to the Customs to go into details of his case history, so I sent it separately.'

'I never received it,' said Kathy, shaking her head. 'But as I am now in charge of him, I came in here tonight to make sure that he had everything he would need until tomorrow, and saw the flowers. I was removing them when you appeared.'

'It's very odd that Becky should do this—*if* she did, as she has been his secretary and very good friend for at least three years, and is devoted to him. Surely she knows what makes him ill by now? He has told me how much he depends on her.'

Kathy tried to keep calm, but her face showed her consternation. 'You don't believe me! You think I had the letter and ignored it. You believe that I brought in these flowers and couldn't care less about my patient. Do you think I *want* him to be ill to justify my being here?' She bit her lip. From his expression she guessed that it was exactly what he thought.

'At least I know now that he is in no danger tonight,' he said grimly. 'Even a small attack isn't a good idea just now. Some of the drugs we would use have side effects in even a strong person, and if his heart began to fibrillate he would be in trouble.'

'I know all that,' said Kathy. 'I looked up each drug that we have here, to make sure that I know what to do if we need an antidote to the effect they might have.'

He stared at her as if trying to decide what she was really like. 'If all you say is true, then I apologise, but seeing you dressed like that makes me forget that you are a supposedly well-trained and qualified nursing sister.' She lowered her eyes before his intense stare and the curious underlying anger. 'Why can't you wear uniform so that I can see you as a nurse, and not as . . . something quite different,' he ended lamely.

'Supposedly?' That one word remained in her mind, but she had no chance to say more as they heard Rebecca's voice outside the door of the suite.

She glanced round the sitting-room and smiled. She walked into the main bedroom and came out quickly, her big blue eyes wary. 'I see that someone has removed the flowers in there. I thought during dinner that they ought to be removed, but I see that someone had the sense to do so.'

'Becky looks after me so well,' said Sir Elliot. 'Always thinking of some little thing to please.'

'It seemed a pity to take them out,' said Kathy, in a firm voice. 'You arranged them so beautifully, Rebecca, but of course, they can't stay here as there are carnations among them and you know the danger of that.' She saw the sudden dislike that the woman couldn't hide, but went on. 'By the way, did you have a letter for me from Dr Raynor? Another letter?' She looked sympathetic. 'Everything was arranged in such a rush that I'm sure you have overlooked it among all your many other commitments.'

'There was no letter,' Rebecca began, then saw that Dr Raynor was still with them, taking in everything that was said and looking puzzled. She laughed, a trill of girlish amusement and childlike apology. 'Oh, silly old me! Do you know, when I saw "Sister-in-charge", I thought it had to go to Beattie's, and I sent it there. I had no idea of its contents,' she said innocently. She pouted. 'Have I done something terrible?'

'Of course not, my dear.' Sir Elliot took her hand. 'You've had so much to do lately. I'm going to bed now, and we'll have a jolly visit to the museum tomorrow, just the three of us, and later you and I can sort out the business I had to leave before I was ill, while these two tramp the streets and get exhausted.'

'I have to collect the syringes tomorrow,' said Kathy, suddenly shy of being alone with the doctor, even if it was out in the streets of Amsterdam in daytime, being shown the sights.

'Fine. He can take you to the clinic and see that they give you good service,' said Sir Elliot.

'There's no need. A friend will bring them here in the morning, and has promised a supply of disposables for as long as you are here,' said Dr Raynor. 'I came here to Amsterdam partly to see you, Elliot, but Johannes wants me to look over his set-up and maybe take some hints back with me for drug rehabilitation. They are using methadone for treatment in heroin addiction during the withdrawal period, but also other drugs that may take over in time.'

'Drugs? Syringes? I really don't want to know,' said Sir Elliot testily. 'Go where you like and don't bother me with details. Just entertain me and make civilised conversation, and make Sister Tyler smile, for heaven's sake. It's not late by your standards. Go for a walk and take these two women with you. I'm ready for bed. I haven't felt better for years, and I don't want people fussing over me just now.' He stopped at the door to his room. 'You aren't going back yet, are you? Dinner tomorrow and a game of Scrabble, if you can bear it? Becky gets very tired of the game, but we never seem to have enough people for Trivial Pursuit.' He laughed. 'Until now! Becky, we'll play that, tomorrow night after dinner. *All* of us,' he said with a note of satisfaction. 'One of the advantages of being sick is that I can be difficult and demand attention.'

'You are a fraud, Elliot, and I can't think why I bother with you. You are fitter than many men half your age, now that you have a freeway round your heart.' Raynor's voice was full of humour and affection. He looked lazily relaxed, and the firm, mobile mouth was gentle. Kathy felt again that he would never show this side of his nature to a woman who was not an old friend, was not a typical nursing sister, and who could not be slotted into a category. She watched his face and her heart beat faster. He was smiling now as if he did know her, had met her before, and was pleased that they had met again.

'My feet are killing me,' said Rebecca. 'If you think I'm going to wander round Amsterdam in the dark wearing these shoes, then you can think again. I didn't bring wellies or flatties, and I hate walking.'

'Quite right, my dear. You have such pretty feet, and we can go everywhere by car tomorrow.' Elliot Russell smiled at her with affection, and she looked pleased. Kathy smothered a smile, but not before an answering one appeared in the eyes of the doctor. For a moment their glances were locked, and she held her breath. He really did have the most compelling eyes she had seen for a long time, and it was good to feel that he had the same opinion of Becky that Kathy had. He looked away and Kathy lost the moment of mutual humour and understanding that the look had shared.

She's half-way to the altar if she is careful, thought Kathy with amusement. No wonder she hated to see another woman on the horizon. She went to change into more suitable shoes, and to pull on the long knitted woollen coat of deep purple that had little to do with the image that Becky had conjured up of beige cardigan and slippers.

There was no escape, as Dr Raynor insisted that he needed a little exercise before going back to his friend's house for the night. He glanced at the simple pale green flat shoes with non-slip soles and the slightly pert bows of dark green suede on the fronts. 'No trainers?' he asked, laughing.

'With this coat?' she said. 'Trainers tomorrow, and then I can lose myself in a crowd of students if necessary.'

'You really want to walk?' he asked. 'Don't let Elliot push you around.'

'I thought that it was you who was being manipulated,' she said. 'There's no need to take me; I can go for a walk alone.'

'By the Amstel, at night? Surely you know that all waterfronts, all over the world, are not places for women to walk alone? You'd be accosted.'

He had not said that he wanted to walk with her, and she felt that he was doing his duty to Elliot more than to her, but as they reached the path by the water she was glad not to be alone. Lights from ships in the distant docks showed briefly between the trees and in the gaps between the houses. The hum of the ever-moving trams came from the busy streets, and the soft slap of the water under a barge came across gently, as if Amsterdam was a place of peace, and she felt safe.

The presence of the now silent man at her side was a wall of security. Maybe he was doing what was expected of any man stuck with a strange woman who knew nothing of the city, and maybe he didn't even like her, but Kathy wished that they could walk side by side like this for hours. They left the water behind and crossed small bridges, saw squares emerge almost in darkness and then bright lights and noise.

'Where are we?' she asked.

'Dam Square to visitors, but the Dutch call it Dam. Here are gathered every type, every race and every age at times. Students meet and exchange news, meet old friends who they know are in Amsterdam somewhere. It's like Piccadilly Circus. They say you meet people there whom you have not met for years, if you hang around for long enough.'

'And be picked up? No, thanks. I've never met a soul I know in Piccadilly. I hurry by and try not to see the junkies,' said Kathy.

'That is here, too,' said Dr Raynor quietly. 'Look over there.' Kathy saw three young men and a girl, lying on the hard ground as if in a deep sleep, except for the violent twitching of one of them. 'There's so much work to do among them, and Johannes gets very dispirited at times, but we are learning all the time.'

Kathy shivered—not because she was cold, but because these people seemed out in a cold, cold world of their own, without hope. 'You seem concerned enough to want to work here, and yet you say that you are only visiting,' she said.

'I'm taking a kind of sabbatical to find out more about how other cities cope with the drug situation and, as I am partly Dutch, it is natural that I am interested in Amsterdam. The fact that I speak Dutch is an advantage, and they welcome any help I can give in return. There is a lot to be done, but we can only cope with so much. If we save just one child it makes it all worth while.' He laughed as if she might think him too evangelical and a fanatic. 'There are personal reasons, too.' Raynor put an arm round her shoulders. 'I'm sorry. You are too tired to see all this tonight. I've walked you too far.' His arm was comforting and she smiled, then denied that she was

cold or tired. 'We'll find some coffee and get the tram
back to Herengracht,' he said. He released her.
'Only,' he said slowly, 'it means taking a short cut
through the red-light district.'

'If I'm with a man, that's no problem, surely, Dr
Raynor?' said Kathy.

'Certainly not, especially if you insist on calling me
that! I'm Michiel. Not Michael, as in English, but
Michiel, after my mother's father. And you are
Katharine?'

'Kathy,' she said. 'Everyone calls me that, except
for my aunt who died last year.'

He tucked her hand under his arm and they walked
slowly across the square. My cousin does this, and it
gives me a warm, protected feeling, Kathy
remembered. She glanced up at the dark profile and
wondered if, for him, this was just a friendly gesture,
but she was far more aware of him than she had been
of any man for a long time. His hand was firm and
almost possessive, as if he was someone she had met
again after a long time—someone who knew her well.

It must be the night sounds of the city that are
affecting me, she thought, the influence of the
transient lights and the colour of the floodlit towers
and the throbbing undercurrent of sexuality that
permeated the square, where couples sat entwined
on wooden benches and on walls, and others walked
side by side as if they had just made love and could
not bear to be parted. Stalls selling hot dogs and soft
drinks still had customers, and they found a small
café where the coffee smelled good. They sat outside
under an awning, almost chilled, but unwilling to go
inside and miss the passing parade of the ever-
moving tide of people.

'Your mother is Dutch?' she asked when they sat in

silence and she had to break a tension she felt
building up between them.

'My mother was born in Rotterdam, but came to
live here soon after she was born, and she lived here
until she married my father. He met her just after the
war, when she was in hospital suffering from
malnutrition, as her childhood was spent under
German occupation here among the shortages of
war.'

'Was he a patient, too?'

'He was a physician sent from England to assess
the numbers of people needing special help. He saw
her and fell in love and took her to Wales, where she
slowly recovered under the care of his family, and
with the fresh farm produce that they could obtain
even when rationing was still in force. They married
two years later when she was eighteen, and later I
was born.'

'He must have loved her very much,' said Kathy.

'Yes,' he said simply. 'He was a lot older than her,
and now she is alone again, but, being the woman
she is, she looks forward and tries to recall only the
good times. I see her fairly often, but she has made a
life of her own and is a very busy lady.'

'No signs of malnutrition in her son,' said Kathy
with a forced laugh. She sensed the bond that had
existed between the man and woman whom she
would never meet, and wished that she could
experience such a deep and abiding love, to have a
man as devoted to her for a lifetime of loving.

'No!' He laughed and showed even white teeth
and a wide and generous mouth. 'I was encouraged
to run wild in the Welsh hills, and rode almost before
I could walk. I played games and found them useful
when I went to medical school. Do you like rugby?'

She shook her head. 'You don't surprise me,' he said. 'A man likes to have a few females shouting encouragement from the sidelines, but I find it difficult to get anyone to stand out in the cold for hours pretending to enjoy it.'

'I have done that when the team at my training hospital played St Thomas's,' she admitted. 'But I can't pretend to know the rules, and I never watch now.'

He called for the bill. 'I know,' he said with a slight grin. 'That's when I first saw you. I was playing for Tommie's, and you wore a ridiculous scarf that reached to the ground, enough to trip you up.'

'That wasn't my scarf. It belonged to . . . one of the team, but as I was freezing I wore it and an extra jacket.'

'You looked blue with the cold,' he said cheerfully. 'I remember thinking that only girls in love would risk hypothermia on such a day.' She sensed the question hovering behind the smile, and her lips were stiff as she tried to sound offhand. Had she been so obvious? The remembered pain was dull now, but she recalled that day, too, even if she had had no idea that she was being watched by another player and not just by Tim, who was becoming more and more difficult to understand, and who had kept her waiting or had missed a few of their dates with excuses that were too pathetic to be believed.

'There were other girls, watching brothers and cousins,' she said, blushing under his intent scrutiny. 'How do you know it was me there? I had a hat pulled down over my face and all that scarf.'

'No girl with beautiful auburn hair wears a scarf of those colours unless she is wearing it for someone. You lost your hat when a gust of wind took it, and it fell in a puddle. You stood in the cold without it, as it was soaking.' He laughed, but his eyes were serious. 'We all remarked on it, as it showed even more dedication, and we wished you were on our side. We even toasted you in the bar when we had showered and changed, but you had gone and we couldn't say hello and bribe you to be our cheer-leader at Tommie's!'

'I had a date,' she lied. Almost true, she recalled. She had thought she had a date, until she had seen Tim with a girl with blonde hair tucked under a big fur hat, who showed all the signs of knowing the handsome doctor extremely well when she walked over to him in the pavilion after the rugby game. She had disappeared when Kathy had emerged from the ladies' room after tidying her wet hair, and there was a message to say that Tim had been called back on duty for an emergency renal failure. When Kathy asked about it later, somehow the case didn't seem to be on the admissions list, and nobody in the ward had heard about a renal crisis that day.

'Let's walk,' he said quietly, as if he wished to forget that he had met her and remembered it so clearly. He thrust the money for the coffee under the bill, and they walked away into the dimly-lit side-road that led to the canal-bank. A brightly lit canal-boat went slowly past, stirring the grey water into soft curls as the banks sent back the wash. Faces from the boat peered at the tall, dark houses, where every window was lit from the back, showing pretty bedrooms, elaborate Victorian boudoirs, and other rooms lit by shaded lights, hinting at black leather and more sinister forms of prostitution.

Kathy quickened her steps. Girls sat or lounged in various states of undress in the rooms, and some of the windows were now covered with thick curtains as customers went in to enjoy sex for sale. Her face burned and she averted her gaze. None of the girls seemed to notice the tourists gazing avidly at the windows, but somehow Kathy knew that she couldn't laugh at this scene—not while she was with this man.

He put a guiding hand under her elbow and led her past the touts and the idlers by the house fronts, and they ran to catch the tram they needed to take them back to the Herengracht. 'I'm sorry about that,' he said.

'I don't know which was the worst—the people really involved, or the voyeurs who stood and gawped at the windows,' she said. 'How can they do it?'

'For many reasons,' he said, almost sternly. 'Some like the life, and others have to earn money somehow, and a pretty face and a good body are valuable currency.'

The tram sighed to a halt and they were once again walking in the peace and elegance of the Herengracht. 'Surely you can't approve?' she asked.

'I find it sad and very dangerous for the girls and for their clients, especially now there is AIDS.' He shrugged. 'It is the oldest profession. We found cures for most of the venereal diseases, and now we shall, in time, find a cure for AIDS.'

'But before that, hundreds will die!' she said, passionately. 'And it still doesn't excuse it.'

'I am a realist,' he said. 'It exists, and the best we can do is to try our best to cure and to educate people against it, but there will always be such places, either in public as we have them here, or in the backstreets in less hygienic surroundings and with more hidden vice than we see here.'

'But don't you care?' They stopped by the wall of the hotel under a street-lamp. 'That isn't love!'

'Of course I care,' he said angrily. 'Love should be sweet and kind and as deep as the sea, but only a few are lucky enough to discover it.' He raised her face between his hands and looked deeply into her eyes, where tears threatened, making dark blue pools of light.

He kissed her gently and her lips wanted to cling in an unfamiliar sweetness, as if she had glimpsed a rose-garden through a half-open door. He put her from him slowly, and the roses faded. 'Tomorrow, at two, precisely,' he said. 'You bring the notebook and I'll bring the guide.'

CHAPTER THREE

'MAY I join you?' The man who stood at least five inches taller than the waiter, who was pushing in the breakfast trolley, smiled.

'Johannes Wittener?' Sir Elliot Russell came to meet him and urged him to sit at the table which had been extended to allow breakfast to be served in the sitting-room of the suite. 'Michiel told me that you might be here this morning.'

Kathy watched the two men and wondered how Michiel Raynor had come to know this huge blond doctor. She smiled. Probably in some terrible rugby scrum when they were both covered in mud, she decided. He saw her smile and turned to her. 'You must be Kathy Tyler. Michiel told me you were here.'

His handclasp was warm and his manner direct, and Kathy liked what she now saw, once the first impression of toughness was past, but the touch of his hand stirred only trust and friendliness and had none of the impact of the man who had kissed her softly and fleetingly last night. His eyes held a deep tiredness, but his mouth smiled and his manner was relaxed, as if he needed to sit for a while and recover from something that had taxed his strength and patience to the limit.

'Coffee?' Rebecca sat behind the enormous coffee-pot as if she was very much in charge, and she smiled at him in a slightly flirtatious way.

'Please. A large cup, two sugars and lots of cream,'

he demanded, and turned back to Kathy. 'You trained at Beattie's? Then you know John Cummings who runs the special clinics.'

Kathy nodded and handed him the cup that Becky held out, and which he had not noticed. 'I never worked with him, but I know of him,' she said. 'Who have you met from other departments?'

He mentioned one or two names and they made a mild attempt at conversation, but as he drank the last of three cups of coffee he yawned. 'I brought enough disposables to last you while you are here, and if you have any queries about drugs or other equipment, call me. Michiel said you have my number.'

'Thank you. I speak very little Dutch and I was dreading having to ask for things at the clinic. Is that where you work?'

'You'll have to come along.' He grinned. 'You look very fit, Sir Elliot. Why do you need a nurse who could be put to much better use with me, where she'd do some good?'

'Because, my dear boy, I have been ill and I need cosseting! I can pay for the best, and the best is what I have!' Johannes laughed, but was obviously slightly irritated. 'You think I'm a self-indulgent fool, but I nearly died, and I intend to enjoy life in the future, knowing that I was nearly finished,' Sir Elliot went on calmly. 'Kathy can come to your clinic one day when I can spare her, but she works for me, and no other, while she is here in Amsterdam.' He slipped into the more intimate use after hearing the visitor call Kathy by her name.

'Well, I have to get some rest. I was up all night and have had no more than five minutes with Michiel since he came back last night,' said Johannes with a stifled yawn.

'I thought that clinics were in the daytime,' said Rebecca. 'I had to make an appointment with one in England when I was ill, and they kept me waiting for what seemed like hours.'

'This is different,' he said. 'We stay open day and night and never refuse anyone. It's run on a voluntary basis, and everyone works very hard.'

'Oh, you mean a casualty department?' she said.

'They are casualties,' Johannes agreed. 'Not necessarily broken bones, although we do get some, but many often sad and very sick and needing help and counsel.' He stretched. 'I'm for bed, and if Michiel asks where I am, tell him to meet me tonight and he'll know where to find me.' He turned to Kathy. 'I take it that Michiel likes his patient to rest in the afternoons? I know that you and Michiel are sight-seeing today, but tomorrow I suggest you come to the clinic and see what we do.'

Kathy looked at Sir Elliot and he nodded. 'Quite the best arrangement,' he said. 'Take every afternoon off, and be free as soon as dinner is over in the evenings, too—unless we play bridge or Trivial Pursuit.'

'I'll ask Michiel to tell me where to find you,' Kathy promised. 'I'd like to see the clinic.'

She waited for the others to finish breakfast, and stacked everything on to the trolley that had brought the food to the suite. She brushed crumbs from the table and removed the cloth, so that Sir Elliot could sit with his books close at hand and she could use a corner for the blood-pressure apparatus, and could do her morning routine of examination of pressure, pulse and respiration. She shook the mercury down in the thermometer and he waved it aside. 'I don't need that any more. My temperature is normal.' She smiled and stood with the slim glass tube in her hand, and he shrugged and accepted it under his tongue, but gave her a mildly exasperated look. Kathy wondered if she was completely unnecessary to his well-being, as his secretary hovered round him everywhere he went and had obviously been very efficient when he was really ill.

'Right,' she said. 'You are normal in every way, as far as I can see. I think I should ring the agency and ask for another job if VSO are still likely to keep me waiting for a posting.'

'I could do that for you,' said Rebecca, rather too quickly.

'No! Michiel said I should keep you here until I am back to my normal working schedule, in case any stress triggers off an attack of asthma.'

'He could be right,' said Kathy slowly. 'But if you have a nurse with you, the tendency will be for you to think you are an invalid even after you are well.'

'I am cheating,' he said. 'I like to know that you will be here if needed, but knowing from our conversations in hospital your family history and Dutch connections, I grabbed you to help me in my work in subjects that would bore my dear Becky to tears. We start today.' He glanced at her sideways, like a boy expecting a reprimand.

'That's a relief,' said Kathy. 'I hate being idle, and yet I am in your employ doing rather less than at any time in my career. If I can visit the clinic and perhaps a hospital while I'm here, I am quite willing to take notes for you and to look up references. I can do some of the leg-work, and you can give the material to Becky to type and to make tidy, as I am not the world's best secretary, and my writing is terrible.'

'That's great!' Becky beamed. 'I like old buildings,

but I can never remember historical facts, and when I do they mean nothing to me.' She gave Kathy a reporter's notebook and a ball-point pen and several guides to the various museums.

'You really do mean to keep me busy,' said Kathy, laughing. 'I think the car will be here in half an hour to take us to Rijksmuseum. I'll carry the briefcase, and it might be chilly unless they have heating on at this time of the year, so bring a warm jacket. Late spring can be cold, and many places switch off heat on the first of May even if it snows.'

'Not where there are valuable paintings. It doesn't matter if the attendants freeze, but they have to care for the canvases and other artefacts.'

'I'll meet you in the foyer, Sir Elliot,' said Kathy. 'I'll make sure that the car has come.'

'Could you bear to call me Elliot? It's more friendly,' he said when they were sitting in the car and being driven slowly across Amsterdam. 'Even if you do leave me, I hope that we shall keep in touch and be good friends. This for me is a holiday, but with a great feeling of safety now that you and Becky are with me.'

'It's a holiday for me, and I shall enjoy helping with your work,' she said, and they spent the morning looking at pictures, finding old manuscripts and studying some of the many historical relics dating from the seventeenth century. Her notes grew as they went from gallery to gallery, and when it was time for lunch and Kathy firmly steered him towards the door and the waiting car, Elliot was flushed and bright-eyed and almost too happy, protesting that he wasn't tired and they could have stayed for at least another hour.

'A light lunch and a good sleep, in bed with no

books,' Kathy said firmly. 'Becky will be with you, as she spent the morning shopping and knows when we shall be back, so you will have company. I have enjoyed this morning very much, and if you want me to take any pictures of houses this afternoon when I'm with Michiel, just tell me what you want.'

She wondered if she sounded too eager to help, but a rush of pleasant anticipation made her laugh softly as if she knew that something wonderful might happen. Michiel would call for her at two, and they would have the entire afternoon together. She felt her lips soften into tenderness. Surely that one tiny kiss had not been just a polite goodnight? The memory had stayed with her until she had slept, and now seemed to be still on her lips.

But an inner voice mocked her. You have been in love, and you were blinded by one man's desire so that you never knew what he was really like until it was too late, it reminded her. This one kiss was nothing more than a touch, a simple 'Hello, I think you're pretty and kissable and nice to know.'

She bit her lip and tried to forget that she had ever been so blind over Dr Timothy Stone, but the memory of his blue eyes . . . such true blue eyes, and that quirky smile that had made her knees turn to water whenever he'd said he loved her . . . now mocked her and told her that all men could put up a show and fake love just to feed their own egos. She frowned. It was possible that she had met Michiel Raynor at some time when the rugby teams met for supper and drinks after matches, but that had been during the time when she had been so obsessed by Tim that she had thought only of him and the need to keep his wandering eyes on her, and her alone.

'Don't worry, darling,' he'd said so many times

that now it seemed as if it had been a built-in, automatic reaction that he must have used with many girls. 'You know that you are the one I really love. I just like women,' he'd said with a little shrug to show it wasn't important. 'When we get married, I promise never to look at another woman, and they will know I am safely caught with the rings we shall exchange, and they'll leave me alone.' He had smiled to show that it wasn't his fault that women ran after him. 'Be fair, Kath, I have to meet a lot of very nice girls and I can't be rude to them, can I?'

And I believed him, Kathy thought, bitterly. I lost my sense of proportion, wasted a lot of time and lost my sense of humour, and all the time I knew in my heart that we would never marry.

It was strange that Michiel Raynor had been there at the match on the very day that she had stormed out of Tim's life forever and applied for a posting with Voluntary Service Overseas, convinced that she had finished with doctors for good. She had gone to Tim's apartment as soon as she was dry and warm again, to return his scarf and to wait for him to surface after the 'emergency' that had never been. Soft laughter from the tiny sitting-room had made her stop by the door. An expensive fur hat had lain discarded on the hall-table. A sweater had lain on the floor, Italian leather boots had made the trail to other garments, and a woman's voice, throaty and passionate, had been saying how much she loved him.

And now? The classical good looks made a blurred image on her memory and the small meannesses and sulky moods made her wonder how she had ever been so blind. She snapped her purse shut. When she had been with Tim she had been under his spell, but now she knew that it had only been a physical attraction, and one she must avoid in the future. That included dark brown eyes and Celtic voices and a chin with an endearing cleft that shouldn't be allowed, and the firm warm grasp of a male hand over hers inside a deep coat pocket while the lights of Amsterdam glowed over the Amstel.

Kathy ate lunch quickly, and changed into jeans and a blue sweater and trainers. The brightness of her hair defied the simple gear, and the soft loose top suggested the gentle fullness of her breasts and slid over her shapely hips. She made sure that Elliot was really in bed, and when she left he was nearly asleep and Becky waved her off as if she was glad to be left to read magazines and to listen to her Walkman radio.

The foyer was empty, as most of the organised trips had started and anyone taking them had left the hotel. Kathy looked at the list of places she wanted to see, and tried to divide the city into four sections so that she could concentrate on one at a time and not miss anything of interest. She looked at her watch, and in the distance could hear the tune played on the hour on the carillon from the Mint Tower, which she knew played a different tune on every half-hour and hour, day and night. She sat away from the door, wanting to see Michiel arrive and have time to compose her face into polite interest, slightly confused by her own eagerness to see him again, a soft smile on her lips; then she began to pace the floor as another half-hour came softly and tunefully from the distant clock.

Kathy tried to study a guidebook and by now was feeling conspicuous. The porter eyed her with interest and she had a feeling that he thought she was one of the local street girls waiting for an assignation.

If he asks me if I'm new here, I'll scream, she thought, then approached the girl in reception and asked if there had been a message for her from Dr Raynor. At least it established the fact that she was really waiting for someone who was late.

Another half-hour went by and she was about to go back to the suite. She decided not to telephone Johannes to ask if he knew where to find Michiel, in case he was still asleep. She looked back from the lift door just as the elevator came to a stop on the floor above and she pressed the button to bring it down. The street door was flung open and Michiel Raynor strode in, looking very angry.

'Oh, there you are!' he said, as if she had kept him waiting. 'Come on, we have work to do.'

'It's after three——' she began.

'I know that. I've a car waiting, and we have to hurry.'

'Where are we going?' she asked when he released her arm and she found herself sitting in a taxi. 'I thought we were going to walk along the canals.'

'Another time,' he said briskly.

'If you are too busy, I can go alone,' she suggested. 'If I'd known that you would be late and obviously rushed, I could have started out at two.'

He sat forward, looking down at his hands. 'I'm sorry if I've interrupted your nice little *holiday*, but this is important,' he said, with an ironic emphasis on holiday.

'I'm not on holiday. I was with Elliot all the morning, and I thought we were to relax this afternoon.'

'And I thought that any nurse from Beattie's would be eager to do some real work instead of wet-nursing a man who has nothing the matter with him.'

'I am here because you ordered a nursing sister to be with him,' she pointed out. 'I had no intention of coming with him when I finished my stint in the private wing with him, but I was persuaded as I had nursed him for a few days and knew him better than most, and for some reason they insisted that it must be me who came with him. I am ready to do any work that is necessary, but when I am off duty I expect to enjoy it and not be attacked by some . . . maniac who can't even keep a date.' She glared at him, her blue eyes dark with sadness. Where was the gentle soul who had held her face in his hands and kissed her?

'I sent you a message,' he said. 'I rang this morning and left a message that you were to find your way to the area called the Jordaan and help me with two patients who were left from the batch that Johannes had to deal with last night.' He made an effort to be calm. 'I asked the receptionist to make a note and put it in the door of Elliot's suite so there would be no delay in you finding it.'

'I had no message,' Kathy said. 'At two-thirty I asked at the desk if there had been a message for me left with the room-key, and the girl looked in the slot and said there had been none.'

'You must have had it. Becky was there at lunch, wasn't she? One of you must have seen it.'

'One of us!' said Kathy bitterly. 'Do you really think I would have sat in that foyer for an hour and a half waiting for you if I'd had a message?'

'I can't believe that Becky would be so forgetful. She is a very efficient secretary, and probably a lot more to Elliot, but that's their business.'

'Well, now I've been hijacked, where are we going? I assume that you take it for granted that I will do whatever you ask, so am I to act as a kind of district nurse, scrub for an operation, or take out stitches?'

'I expected you and it's put us all out,' he complained.

'I'm very sorry,' she said coldly. 'Who was put out and why? I'm only the *un*paid *un*volunteer who doesn't have to know what's going on, but is expected to come when you call! I could take a taxi straight back, pack my bag and leave Holland tomorrow! You say that Elliot doesn't need me, and I agree. I could do more good back in the theatre at Beattie's, where I was treated with a little respect.' The tears that she held back were hot, and all the more painful because she had hoped that he was different from other men who had tried to make demands of her.

'Kathy . . .' he began, but she turned her head away and stared out of the window. Glimpses of bright water and the poignant droop of slender branches over the canals made it even more difficult to hold back the tears, and she sat stiffly and as far away as she could from the man who had seemed to want to be her friend. 'I'm sorry,' he said. 'I was angry and I was wrong to be, but this morning has been very frustrating and I hoped that you could help us out.'

'Well, we seem to have arrived somewhere,' she replied ungraciously, then laughed. 'It can't be here! I just don't believe it.' The taxi stopped outside a tall house that had once been handsome, but now lacked a few coats of paint on the maroon window-ledges. The stonework was shabby and the front door was open on to a dimly lit interior that smelled of stale food and disinfectant. Children played in the muddy lane that ran beside the house, and a refuse box overflowed by the front door. 'Real district nursing,' she said drily, but she was losing her anger and now finding this an adventure. 'Reminds me of midwifery in Glasgow and health-visiting in Birmingham.'

'You haven't seen anything yet,' promised Michiel and glanced at her with relief to see the laughter in her eyes. 'I hope all your clothes are washable!'

'Tell me, what are Dutch fleas like?' she asked.

'They bite,' said Michiel, 'but they only like luscious women and leave us men alone.'

'Thank *you!* That makes it all worthwhile,' she said. Michiel led the way through the passage to the back of the building where windows opened on to the canal. A woman rose from a battered chair and smiled faintly, eyeing Kathy without curiosity. Michiel spoke in Dutch and the woman replied, shrugging and showing no concern.

'What did she say?' asked Kathy, who sensed that Michiel was alarmed.

'Her daughter is a drug addict and pregnant. This morning we brought her out of a near coma, and told her to wait here until we could find a hospital bed for her where they could dry her out properly. There was more chance of a bed as she is pregnant, but the girl has now disappeared.'

'What is this place?' asked Kathy. 'Is this her home?'

'The woman lives next door and holds the key to this house. We have a clinic here twice a week for people who will not come to hospital, but we try to have someone here all the time, and volunteers cook soup and simple meals for any who need help. Upstairs, in a room we keep locked, we have a small theatre and equipment, and a few mattresses for recovery in another room. A lot of addicts have abscesses that have to be opened and minor injuries that occur because they sometimes fall over or run into things when they are nearly blinded from a fix of heroin. Last night Johannes had six cases here, and we can never send them away or they'll stay away and maybe end up in a canal. Come on, I have two more up there, and I need help with them.'

Kathy followed him up the narrow stairs in a daze. She was even more confused when he unlocked a door and she saw a brightly lit room that smelled of cleanliness and disinfectant. A cupboard with a heavy padlock sat against one wall, and a tray of instruments was ready for a minor incision. He handed her a white coat and showed her where to scrub her hands. 'But you should scrub,' she protested. The whole situation was opening out like a bad dream. 'You are the doctor!'

'I have to make sure he stays on the table,' he said grimly. 'I can't give him any more drugs, and he will hardly feel a thing, I hope!'

'You haven't locked him up?'

Michiel laughed heartily for the first time since they met that afternoon. 'You can't have forgotten Casualty on a Saturday night? It must have been the same at Beattie's as it is with us. When they are out cold, it would take a bomb to wake them. No, he was out cold just now and I had time to fetch help, but he's a big boy and powerful and I couldn't open the abscess and hold him at the same time if he *did* feel it.'

'You don't expect me to open the abscess?'

'Of course. You've done as much in Cas, haven't you? A few stitchings, and even more when a big accident came in, like the rail disaster.' He smiled as if they shared the same memory, but surely he couldn't have been there, even if he had heard all about it? Again, she had the uncanny sensation that he knew her, and that he had watched her in many situations of which she was ignorant.

She turned so that he couldn't see her face. How could he know about that time when the whole of the hospital had seethed with urgency and all the beds had been filled, even in the corridors where more had been hastily erected? Both tables in the small theatre usually reserved for dental and eye work had been in use, with two surgical teams trying not to get in each other's way. She gulped as the scene came back so vividly that she could almost hear the surgeon shouting for her to take the place of the house surgeon who had fainted. She had stitched five incisions that night, and been first assistant to two more, as the mangled limbs had been straightened and cleansed and made as nearly whole as possible.

'You weren't there?' she asked in wonder. 'They were brought in to us and to three other hospitals, but not to any hospitals across the river.'

'St Thomas's was alerted, and we came as fast as we could and took over for the next day, as you lot had been working for twelve hours non-stop.' A tiny pulse throbbed in his cheek and his laughter was forced as they stood and looked at each other. He turned away. 'You looked like a zombie,' he said, almost cheerfully, 'but you'd left very little between you for us to clear up. You must have worked like hell.'

A faint blush crept over her face, and she was glad to be wearing a mask. She scrubbed her hands well and pulled on the rather thick surgical gloves that he indicated. 'I can't feel a thing through these,' she grumbled, glad to have something to say.

'Just don't tear them or prick yourself through

them,' he said urgently. 'You never know where our patients have been! Hepatitis is bad enough, but now we have *AIDS*.'

'Thanks very much!' Kathy stood ready with the scalpel lined up with a row of swabs, and eyeless needles with sutures attached clamped in three needle-holders so that she would lose no time fixing a fresh needle for use. Scissors were ready, and a small bowl of antiseptic skin-paint held two swabs ready for use.

'I'll spray the surface, and then you cut across where I have put a mark with a ball-point pen,' said Michiel. 'If he isn't stroppy, I can help you sew up, but if you see that I have my hands full, get on with it. If you can insert a small drain, all the better, but I doubt if we have time and, in any case, it might lead to infection. No, leave the drain. Just make sure you don't sew up one end too tightly, then the discharge can get away. He'll have to have a massive dose of antibiotics and hope that this will prevent any secondary infection, as his tissues are in very poor condition. This is almost certainly staphylococcal and resistant to most antibiotics, but I'm more concerned with what might get into the wound if he leaves here and doesn't have it dressed.' He glanced at the needle-holders and grinned. 'I can see that you have had restless football fans with cuts that had to be sewn up fast in Casualty.'

For a moment, Kathy felt a warmth between them again, and it gave her courage to face the man whom Michiel almost dragged in and sat on the reclining dental-chair that was more convenient for this case. He strapped the man's arm to a rest attached to the side of the chair and grinned. The face was flabby and very pale, the slack mouth was half-open and his

breathing was heavy and slow. Michiel sprayed the
arm with lignocaine solution. The man grunted and
clenched his hand, but soon relaxed. 'I can't give
anything more or it will add to his condition. This is
the most suitable of the local anaesthetics that we can
use, and even then we have to be careful because of
toxic absorption,' Michiel said, then nodded. 'Be
quick and do it with one cut.'

Kathy took a deep breath, and braced herself. I
shall have to do far more than this if I go with VSO,
she told herself in one last effort to be strong, and,
outwardly calm, she did as Michiel directed while he
held on to the hand and arm rest, as soon as the man
began to struggle. The first stitch went in, and Kathy
almost gagged at the smell of the discharge from the
abscess. She swamped the wound with cleansing
hydrogen peroxide solution, and put in the next
suture. It went in slightly askew, but it would hold
fast, and the third almost missed the incision as the
man tried to get out of the chair. Kathy now knew
why she had the easier task of making a simple cut
and stitching. Michiel had to use all his strength to
keep the man still.

'Leave it like that and flood the wound with the
dilute hydrogen peroxide solution again. Good! He'll
do!'

Kathy mopped up the fluid and saw the skin edges
become clean through the froth of the clean-smelling
peroxide. She applied a firm dressing and encased
the arm in a cylindrical stockingette bandage. 'Do
you think that will keep clean?' she asked doubtfully.

'No, in two days it will be filthy and he will try to
use that arm for injecting, but what can we do? This
abscess will heal, but there will be others, and when
he collapses in the street, then he may get taken into

hospital. The hospital service here is fine, but the problems in any big city—and that includes London, Paris, Berlin and New York—are the same, and of such proportions that they can't do without such places as these and our St Martin's Crypt and societies like the Cyrenians in London.'

'You said there were two cases,' said Kathy, and she filled the small sink with water and strong disinfectant and washed the instruments carefully before taking off her gloves. 'Where do I sterilise these?' she asked. He showed her a small fish-kettle on a gas ring, and she put a few swabs in the bottom before lowering the clean instruments into the boiling water, to prevent the instruments from contacting the sides while boiling.

'The other case went to hospital. I diagnosed an acute abdomen, and not the stomach-ache that sometimes goes with the effort to do without drugs. Johannes is apt to see everyone as a potential addict or a prostitute, as he works among them so much.' Michiel gave a faint smile when Kathy looked shocked. 'Come now, didn't you, when you started nursing, sit on the top of a bus and diagnose everyone in sight according to which ward you were working on at the time?'

Kathy relaxed. 'It's quite true. I was sure that at least three people had an enlarged thyroid after seeing one for the first time in Ward Nine, until one of the house surgeons pulled off his tie, showed me his Adam's apple and said that all men had larger tracheas than women, and that in old portraits of women a plump neck with a slight swelling in the throat was very attractive to the men of the time, and they had no need of surgery!'

'How times change. The emphasis is on a very

different part of the body now, I believe.' He looked
at her with a mocking smile. 'Elliot likes pretty feet,
and can't wait for high-heeled sandals with ankle-
straps to come back into fashion, and some men
prefer legs or breasts or hips.' Kathy blushed and
turned away, glad that the straight white coat hid her
body, but aware that her jeans were tight in all the
right places. She had absolutely no intention of
asking what turned the doctor on! 'With those
trainers, Elliot wouldn't approve of the feet, but the
rest is fine,' he said lightly. 'Come on, I'll tell the
woman downstairs to give him a cup of coffee in an
hour when the local begins to wear off, and then he'll
vanish until the next time. Help me with him on to
the mattress in the other room.'

Kathy looked at her watch. 'We must wait for
another quarter of an hour to make sure the
instruments are sterile.'

'They'll have to go into the cupboard and be re-
sterilised before use. We have so few drums that we
need them all for dressings, and have to use the old
ways to sterilise instruments, as you have seen,'
Michiel told her.

'And what if someone comes in and has to use
something in an emergency before they are boiled
again? We can't risk cross-infection when there is no
need for it.'

'Grab that arm and I'll hold the sore one,' was all
he said, but he was smiling, and Kathy was aware of
a kind of tenderness in his eyes. They went back into
the surgery and Kathy swabbed the floor with a mop
heavily impregnated with disinfectant that soon
killed the smell of the abscess, and then she opened
the cupboard door to inspect the rest of the
equipment, which was adequate for a small casualty-

theatre. 'Are all these really surgically clean?' she asked.

'I have no idea. I came here first last year to visit Johannes and he made me promise to come back, so when Elliot was recovering and I knew where he wanted to convalesce I decided to take time to come here again at the same time.' He paused as if unwilling to say more, then added, 'I had other business here, too, of a personal nature.'

'I see.' Kathy thought back to the sight of Michiel wearing the over-bright and rather vulgar tie. It must be very personal, she thought.

She felt his hands on her shoulders and the warmth of his fingers made her want to turn to him, but she stiffened and shrugged out of her white coat, leaving it in his hands, as if she took it for granted that this was his intention and nothing more, but her flesh tingled where he had touched her and she knew that he wanted to kiss her.

'Thank you,' she said, and glimpsed an expression of disappointment as he took the coat and hung it on a hook by the door. 'I'll wash again now, as it will take a while to get the smell from my nostrils. I wish this soap was scented. It's almost as bad as the smell.'

'Use some of this.' From his pocket he produced a small bottle, shaped like a flower, and Kathy recognised it as the scent bottle design used by a very expensive perfume factory.

She held it in her hand and cautiously removed the stopper. The scent rose to the air and she rubbed a tiny spot of it on her wrists, waved her hands around to rid the scent of its spirit, and then sniffed. The perfume was heavy and musky with a sensuality that was foreign to her taste, as she had worn only light flower perfumes, and fresh colognes in hot weather. She sniffed again. It was heady, and she could imagine it being worn by a woman who wanted to dull the senses of a man and encourage him to make love to her.

'Don't you like it?' Michiel asked. 'I thought that all women adored expensive perfume.'

'I can't wear that during the day,' she said. 'It's an after-eight scent, and besides, it's far too tarty for me. Now, if I wore that and waited for you for an hour or so in the foyer of the hotel, I'd have only myself to blame if someone tried to pick me up.'

She glanced at him as they walked down the stairs and she laughed, but he looked very embarrassed and went ahead of her to tell the woman below what to do with the patient.

'It's too late for sightseeing,' he said when he came out into the sunlight. 'I'm sorry there was a misunderstanding, and perhaps we can walk some other time.' His tone was formal and Kathy could feel the ice forming between them.

'If I stay that long in Amsterdam,' she said. 'I think that tram takes us back to Dam Square, and I'd like to walk from there. Please don't bother to come with me. I might see more alone, and I'd hate to take you out of your way.'

She ran to catch the tram, and sank down into a seat, breathless. A man sitting next to her eyed her with interest, and smiled as if to start a conversation, but she didn't like the look in his eyes. She could smell the scent as it warmed in the tram, and she was glad to escape into the fresh air again and to walk briskly, looking neither to right nor left until she arrived back at the hotel.

'Did you have a good time?' asked Becky, who was

in the foyer, as if she had to come down for something from the desk. 'I found this after you left,' she said, and handed over the message that had come that morning. Kathy knew that she was lying.

'That's all right. Michiel came to fetch me,' she said, and didn't add that he was an hour and a half late and in a flaming temper. 'We had a lovely time, and he gave me this perfume,' she said, suddenly realising that she had slipped the flask into her bag and forgotten it.

She held out her hand and Becky sniffed. 'It's the new one and costs the earth,' she said with envy. 'A lot of girls would do a great deal to have that as a gift.'

'Oh, I did,' said Kathy, smiling. 'We went to a house in the Jordaan and spent a very interesting afternoon.'

'But the Jordaan is the place where all the artists and hippy types live,' said Becky.

'It's coming up in fashion,' Kathy assured her. 'But it could do with a sweeter smell, so I have perfume.' She made for the lift. 'How is Elliot? And what does he want to do this evening? I'm starving.' Becky stared at her, open-mouthed, and for a moment Kathy regretted her off-beat remarks that had obviously made Becky believe that something *very* interesting had happened between the two medics on their afternoon off, but she stifled a giggle. It was worth it to see the woman's shocked expression and, looking back, the afternoon had certainly had its hilarious moments.

CHAPTER FOUR

'I HAD the first real deep sleep that I've had for weeks when Michiel took over,' said Johannes. 'Since two volunteers left and my partner had to go into hospital with an ear infection, query mastoid and possibly for operation, I have been desperate for helpers.'

Rebecca looked up at him with sympathetic blue eyes. 'You mean in the hospital? Surely there must be lots of girls willing to help you? I'd come myself if I was free, but I have my own work to do,' she said with an air of being overloaded with heavy tasks.

Johannes laughed as if she had made a very funny joke. 'Not the hospital,' he said. 'Didn't Kathy tell you about her adventures?'

'Becky isn't a nurse,' said Kathy quickly. 'She wouldn't have enjoyed it, and may we change the subject, as it's getting near to dinnertime?' He grinned and walked over to Elliot, who was trying to listen to the results of a horse-race on the radio.

'And what does Becky have to be sheltered from?' the woman asked sarcastically. 'It couldn't be that you don't want Elliot or me to know exactly what went on that afternoon when you came back reeking of scent?' Becky looked at Kathy with calculation. 'Maybe even Johannes doesn't know what happened. Maybe he thinks you were working in his old clinic, giving out advice and medicines, and all the time you were with Michiel in some hotel bedroom!'

Kathy stifled a giggle. 'If you must know, we opened

a very nasty abscess, and cleaned up a surgery after it.'

'You can't fool me,' said Becky with dignity. 'I knew at once that you were not fit to look after Elliot, and now I know for certain.'

'Is that why you held back the message from Michiel and I had to wait for him for over an hour when he expected me to help him with his patients?' Kathy asked softly. 'Yes, I do know it was your fault. I asked the receptionist who was on duty at the time, and she actually said she gave you the message.' Kathy looked serious. 'I'm tired of you trying to get rid of me, Rebecca. I have nothing against you, and I wouldn't stay with Elliot for more than a week or so even if he asked me. I have other plans, and there is nothing here in Holland to keep me. I helped in the clinic because I had to do so, as there was no other person available, and yes, Michiel gave me the scent, but it wasn't bought for me, as the seal was already broken, so I suppose it belonged to some other girl. It wasn't intended for me, but it did take away the awful smell of that place.'

'I'm sorry,' said Rebecca. 'I can't help myself. I get so jealous if another woman is around, and I am afraid that Elliot will never marry me. Don't call me Rebecca! I know that I'm in trouble when anyone calls me that, and it's so ageing.'

'He's more likely to want to marry you if he is really fit,' said Kathy shrewdly. 'I can help with that, and you can just continue to look good and be nice to him, and you do keep his papers in very good order, so he does depend on you in many ways.' She smiled. 'Has he decided what to do this evening?' She sounded politely interested, but could feel no real enthusiasm for any plans that Elliot might have made. Since she had run to catch the tram and left Michiel, two days ago, she had seen nothing of him and heard nothing until Johannes had arrived for drinks this evening and said that Michiel had been working very hard at the clinic, and today had visited Rotterdam.

'I think we could go out,' said Elliot, as if he intended visiting the North Pole, or somewhere equally unlikely for a man who liked little exercise and no effort and certainly no discomfort. 'Ring down and see if we can book dinner on a barge. I feel like some nightlife, and if Johannes will come, too, we can be a nice party.'

'I have never been on one of the tourist barges,' admitted Johannes. 'You will find that many Dutch have never seen the bulb fields or a windmill unless they pass them in the train, and they look on canal-barge trips as something for the tourists.'

'And few Londoners visit the Tower of London or the Abbey,' said Kathy. She laughed. 'I'm a fraud! I try to convince visitors that I know much more than I do, but one American nearly caught me out, and I sat up late the night before I had to take her to see the sights of London. It's humiliating when they come over and know more than we do,' she confessed. 'They expect us to know everything, and have so many good guidebooks that very often I feel ignorant.'

'A pity that Michiel is otherwise engaged,' said Elliot. 'He never tells me what he does when he leaves here. Yesterday he popped in to see that I was all right, and wouldn't stay to say hello to the girls.' He eyed Kathy severely. 'You haven't upset him, have you? He went off in a great hurry.'

'He had a train to catch,' said Johannes, and winked at Kathy as if it couldn't possibly be true, but it would stop Elliot being too curious.

Johannes knows where he is, she thought. Johannes knows about Michiel, and must know about the woman in his life—a woman who gives him vulgar ties and for whom he carries musky romantic scent, a woman who lives in Amsterdam or in some other part of Holland which he can easily visit, but a woman whom he doesn't bring here to be introduced to Elliot. She felt vaguely let down, as if Michiel should have stayed to see her and not, as Elliot said, left in a hurry as if he wanted to avoid her altogether.

'Is Rotterdam a good place to sightsee?' asked Becky hopefully, as she had seen all the smart dress-shops in Amsterdam and the few places that really interested her, like the Anne Frankhuis where Anne Frank and her family had hidden for two and a half years from the occupying Nazi forces before being betrayed to them, and the smaller museums showing old interiors of houses and the clothes worn in bygone days.

'There is a good hospital there and several museums, and it is a fine town,' said Johannes with a wicked smile. 'Many churches and monuments—enough to fill several days.'

'Is that all?' Becky looked disappointed.

'Very good shops, and it is close to Delft where the blue and white Dutch pottery is made. You can see it in progress and buy at reasonable prices,' said Johannes, relenting, and went on to tell her more about the shopping areas there. He mentioned fine lace and linen, and the pretty Dutch national costumes that many tourists bought to take home for fancy-dress parties and carnivals.

'I shall forbid you to buy clogs,' said Elliot. 'They would be too heavy for your feet, and would make your heels sore.'

'They give all who wear them slim ankles,' said Johannes. 'Not that either of you needs to wear them, but the girls who do wear them usually have very fine legs and ankles.'

A message from reception told Elliot that there was a free table for four on one of the canal-barges and they could go there at once, walking across the square to the bridge where the boats were moored.

The night was fine and clear, and a light breeze from the water made the leaves shimmer in the light of the tall street-lamps. The carillon of the clock bells came softly across to them with yet another tune, and a distant street organ added its melody in a way that meant Amsterdam and no other city that Kathy had known, and she wished that she could be alone with someone who would tuck her hand under his arm and draw her close, not talking a great deal, but wandering the side-roads by the canals and taking in the seventeenth century magic. Would she hear that sound in her dreams long after she left Amsterdam?

A boy and a girl in almost identical denim walked slowly towards them, locked in each other's arms, and other couples sat by the water, lost in their own private worlds.

Kathy looked away, and even with the other three in her party she felt isolated, as if her world had lost all warmth and sensuality. Johannes eyed her with interest. They had been side by side on the way to the boat, and now sat together, as Becky wanted to sit next to Elliot. 'Michiel told me that you did very well at our house,' he said. 'You will come again?' He sounded curious rather than anxious. 'I have two helpers now, a man who was an army medical orderly, and a girl who has done some work in a home for the mentally retarded, and another doctor has agreed to come for a month until Hans is better and can resume his duties.'

'Then you don't need me,' she said.

'No, that's true in one sense, but there are women

who might be helped if you could talk to them about hygiene and health in general. Most people speak English here, so that need not worry you. Ignorance is a terrible thing, and many of the women who work the streets have to take great risks and could be encouraged to use barriers and to have regular checks of blood and to receive treatment for the early signs of venereal disease.'

'Surely you don't want me to examine prostitutes while I am working for Elliot? He would go mad if he thought I brought infection back here, and that's why I said nothing about the afternoon I spent with Michiel, as we treated a very dirty case which would have made him very upset if he'd known about it. There are special clinics for VD here, surely, as there are in England? In London I have a shock each time I see a notice in a public lavatory listing my old training hospital as one where confidential and special treatment can be given, and, as I told you, I have never worked in the special clinics where patients have only numbers, and names are never divulged to anyone who might ask about them, to give them complete privacy.'

'As Michiel probably explained, there are many who will never attend a clinic under the State, although we make good provision for them. They are not junkies and just earn their living in the way they best know,' he said simply. 'He is very good with them, and I wish he was here for more than a visit, but he likes London and his old hospital too much to live far away from it all.'

'You sound as if you approve of them!'

'Michiel and I and many others in our profession are realists. A situation doesn't disappear because we approve or disapprove. It exists, and has to be taken as fact and treated in the best way we can. I know women who are really pleasant and very lovely, who know no other life, and have families to support.'

'There are other ways of earning a living.'

'It pays and the girls are used to it quite soon. If men pay for sex, there may be other, more innocent girls and women who are not molested because there are these . . . outlets.'

'What of love?' Kathy asked in a soft voice, almost to herself.

'Love? Do you believe in love? I suppose you do.' Johannes gave a cynical laugh. 'How refreshing! In my job, we see it rarely, but it is there sometimes between a girl and her own man, and some have children whom they love most fiercely and protect from the life they live as much as possible.'

He put a hand over hers where it rested on her lap. The waiter arrived with the wine list for Elliot to pore over and and choose what they should drink. 'Love is a luxury that many of us cannot afford,' said Johannes quietly. 'If I am attracted to a woman, I say so, and if she is willing, I go with her.' He grinned. 'No, don't look like that. I am not so hard up that I have to pay for it yet! I never use my patients. I know the risks far too well.'

He patted her hand and left it, and reached for the menu. 'Thank you,' said Kathy as the waiter poured some wine for her. She studied the menu and tried to forget what Johannes had said, but a nagging thought haunted her. Michiel was Johannes' friend and colleague, used to the hard world of vice through his visits to Amsterdam and his work in London. Did that mean that he was immune to real love, and thought, as his friend did, that women were for appeasing the sexual appetites of men and could be taken and discarded when the need was over? At least Tim had been less cynical about love, and had wanted her friendship and company, and could be very romantic. She knew instinctively that even he, with his roving eye, wouldn't take a woman whose name he didn't know and sleep with her for a brief gratification of lust.

'Don't worry, I know you aren't the type,' he whispered. 'If I thought you would, I'd ask you, but I know when a girl will or will not. One day you will do all the conventional things and marry for keeps,' he said, with a hint of derision.

'Do all doctors see life as you do?' she said, and sipped her wine to take away the dryness of her mouth. 'Does none of you believe in love?'

'I can't speak for them. Maybe they think they will find a woman who will be faithful forever. Maybe some do find her, but it's not for me.' He handed her a serving spoon and held a dish of vegetables for her. 'Once, it might have been, and when I meet girls like you I wonder, but in my heart I know it would take a miracle to make any difference to our lives, and we just do what we can and take what is offered. On the whole I have a good life.'

'And Michiel? Does he have a good life?' she asked, but Johannes only grinned as if the old-boy pact was not to be broken and she would get no information from him about his friend.

'You have been whispering for the past quarter of an hour,' said Elliot.

'Not whispering,' said Johannes. 'Just talking about medical matters, and I know you don't want to hear them.'

'Not a good subject,' Elliot agreed. 'Tell us more about yourself, Johannes. Where do you live?'

'And tell us something about Michiel,' said Becky, with a glance at Kathy.

'I live where my work takes me, mostly in

Amsterdam. I keep a small apartment here and use it, and some of my friends stay there if they are in Amsterdam.'

'Michiel is staying with you now?' asked Becky. 'I suppose he can take his own friends there, too?' she asked with an air of studied innocence.

'He has a key,' Johannes agreed. He shrugged. 'Sometimes the flat is empty for weeks, and then maybe I have people with sleeping-bags on the floor, as each of the two spare rooms are full suddenly, but it's pleasant to accommodate old friends. We make pancakes and doughnuts and curry, and drink far too much cheap wine, but it's like our student days and very nostalgic.'

'You recall old friendships, and all the people you loved?' suggested Becky.

'Those of us, like Michiel and a few more, who have a lot in common and still believe in certain ethical values.'

'Is he very moral?' asked Becky, as if she wanted to share a joke about a man who was a bit too strait-laced.

'It depends what you mean. He hates vice and drugs and everything to do with that kind of life, but he sees the need to help,' said Johannes. 'A bit of a monk at times, but one of the best doctors I know, and I wish he would come to live here for good. He likes to come and help, but I know his real work is at St Thomas's, and this short sabbatical is enough for him as a break after getting his Fellowship, while he waits to see if he's been given the job for which he applied, as registrar.'

'A monk? I wouldn't agree.' Elliot laughed. 'I am sure that Michiel has all the right responses to women, just as I have. What do you think, Kathy? You were with him for an entire afternoon, and walked the canal-banks with him the first night we were here.'

'He was . . . polite, but seemed to resent the fact that I was doing so little work. He made me help him in Johannes' clinic and I haven't seen him since, so I can't say that we have been together socially for time enough to form an opinion,' she said stiffly. And he certainly showed no eagerness to see me again, she thought, with the feeling that the small bottle of scent was the key to his change of mood. 'A pity. I thought you got on rather well,' said Elliot. 'More wine? I can't say much for the food, except for the pudding which does look rather good.'

'Apple pancakes?' Kathy looked across at the next table. 'Pancakes are a special Dutch treat, aren't they? I think I'll have one, but the people over there are having rich chocolate ice-creams with nuts and things.'

'Have both,' suggested Elliot. 'You are far too slim, and need building up. I'm sure that we shall want to taste both of them.'

'Just a pancake,' said Kathy firmly, but smiled and nodded when she was offered cream. 'No pancake for you?' she asked Johannes.

'When you've had as many Dutch pancakes as I have, you'll choose fruit salad,' he said. 'Pancakes were easy to make and were filling during the shortages of war, and have become a part of our diet because of it.'

'This is delicious,' said Kathy. 'I'll go Dutch any time.'

'That means sharing, if I remember my English idiom,' said Johannes. He reached across and helped himself to a piece of her pancake. 'Have some fruit from my dish,' he said, and gave a wicked grin. 'There are so many things we could share, Kathy. Don't keep it all to yourself. Why don't we really "go Dutch" and share everything?'

'Let's stick to food,' she said, and giggled. It was easy

to laugh with Johannes, knowing that he was only half serious and was no threat even when he found her attractive.

The candles burned slowly in the covered barge and, when the dishes were cleared and Elliot ordered liqueurs, she sat back and gazed out of the window at the passing scene. It was strange to see the now familiar sights by night, and some seemed even more clear under the lamps on the canal-banks and the floodlighting of the many bridges. Skinny Bridge lay across the stream, with its outline marked by hundreds of bright light bulbs, and the gaunt shapes of half-built boats loomed above them in the shipyards. There was magic in the air. Over there was where she had leaned on a bridge with Michiel and listened to the carillon softly reminding them of the passing time, his face close to her hair and the smell of his aftershave, masculine and clean.

If only she were here with him now, even if he was still annoyed with her for some reason of which she knew nothing. If it had been Johannes who had that bottle of scent, he would have laughed about it, and she could have dismissed it from her mind, but now her thoughts went back again and again to Michiel's annoyed face, as if the scent bottle was important and something about which she would not want to know. Under the buzz of conversation and laughter, she was lonely. He could have told her to please herself if she wore it or not, and that scent was an individual choice, and if she didn't care for this one, then bad luck! It wasn't necessary to look so embarrassed when she had said it was a bit tarty.

She felt suddenly guilty. She had slipped the glass flower-shaped phial into her bag, and maybe Michiel hadn't had the nerve to ask for it again, but nevertheless wanted it for the woman for whom he had bought it.

Kathy opened her bag and found the scent bottle. She held it in her hand and wished that she could throw it from the sealed window and pretend that she had not taken it from the clinic, but that was absurd. Michiel must have seen her take it, and who but her could have done so? Her nervous fingers fiddled with the cap and it turned slightly. Hastily, she screwed it back, but not before a drop of the potent liquid had found her fingers.

Johannes leaned towards her. 'You smell nice. In fact, you smell very alluring, Kathy. I've met that perfume before, and it's dynamite. A real turn-on! Do you carry it with you all the time?' He looked surprised. 'Somehow I would have said you might prefer flower perfumes and Old English scents, like lavender.'

'It isn't mine. Michiel gave it to me to take away the smell in the clinic, and I forgot to give it back. Could you take it for him?'

'No! Keep it away from me. I could give people the wrong idea if I smelled of that! Don't tell me that my dear old Michiel tried to seduce you with such a gift?' He seemed amused.

'Of course he didn't,' said Kathy, and shut her bag again, hoping that the scent would die away quickly.

'Well, he gave it to you, and obviously wouldn't want it back again. He's not that mean! What did you expect? That he'd give you a dab behind the ear each time he met you and take the bottle away again?'

'It wasn't like that. It had been opened, and it wasn't a gift,' she said, aware of the silent curiosity of Elliot and Becky who seemed entranced by the conversation.

'It's a lovely perfume,' said Becky enviously. 'If you don't want it, I could use it.'

'It's a bit . . . intense,' Kathy said.

Johannes laughed. 'She means it smells like a boudoir. It reeks of sex and seduction, and, being the nice little English girl that she is, she shies away from it, as if it might bite her.'

Becky fluttered her eyelashes at Elliot, and he took her hand. Kathy managed a rueful smile. At least it was having the required effect on two people. If it helped Becky to her heart's desire, she was welcome to it all! She looked out of the window again as several of the passengers were laughing and pointing. The trees hid the tops of the buildings and the canal-bank was dimly lit, but the houses were not in darkness. Kathy recalled the apologetic tone in Michiel's voice when he had led her through the red-light district and the warm touch of his arm holding hers, firm and reassuring, and with an urgency to make her leave the area quickly. She smiled. He cared enough to save her from the sights that might upset her, of women flaunting their sexuality in windows to attract men and trade for their bodies.

From the boat, the scene was even more clear, and certainly taken at greater leisure than if she had been walking past the houses, and the boat slowed down to give the passengers a good look at the many bright windows, each with its set piece of a room with a scantily dressed woman in it, waiting for offers. Kathy stated, fascinated in spite of her own feelings of repulsion. A girl dressed in a scarlet cutaway one-piece swim-suit stood in an open doorway talking to a man, and they both went into the house. A window was suddenly darkened by a thick curtain on the first floor, and another man knocked on the door of the same house. He stood back and looked up at a girl who was dressed in a long pale blue gown, who waved and gestured to another older woman in the background, who left the room, and appeared at the front door a minute later.

Kathy felt as if her heart turned to ice. The light from the front door shone directly on to the man's face and he was smiling. As if the picture was captured on camera, Kathy saw his face and the smile that she had come to visualise with a kind of wistful longing even when Michiel was far away. But this smile was genuinely full of pleasure and anticipation, and not the frowning disapproval that he had shown to her at times, or the embarrassed expression when it seemed that she had said something to make him want to leave her.

Michiel Raynor stepped into the house just as the barge went on, and the window of the room where the pretty blonde in blue waited was lost, hidden behind the trees.

Johannes glanced at her sharply. 'Oh, you did see him,' he said in a flat voice. 'And you've jumped to the wrong conclusions.' She shook her head. Of course they would try to cover for each other whatever happened. Men were loyal in their own way when it came to matters of sex, and if the doctors were closely involved with such women in the course of their duty, then why not take some of the rewards offered as well?

She felt a wave of nausea threatening, but she took a firm grip on herself. How could he? He knew the risks! And what if he made love to another girl who had no idea what he had done with such women, and so put an innocent woman at risk of infection? She took a deep breath. This was ridiculous, and she was mad to have such thoughts, even in a moment of shock. It was impossible! He was a sane and professional man, and the touch of his lips on hers had not been that of a practised lecher. She recovered her senses. Johannes was right. It wasn't what it seemed to be . . . But he had gone into that house! He had recognised the woman, so he knew her! It wasn't the first time he had been there! he shut her eyes for a moment, and then tried to relax and smile, even with her emotions shaken and her memory of him tarnished.

'Did you see that?' Becky sounded very amused and half shocked. Kathy's heart sank. So they would all know about Michiel! He couldn't have been more in the public gaze if he'd gone there in a floodlit car. In fact, he had walked into the house quite openly, as if he cared nothing for what anyone might think.

'What did you see that was so awful?' said Johannes, with the bored expression of a man who has seen it all, but Kathy sensed that he didn't want everyone to know what Kathy and he had seen.

'Why, that woman in the ground-floor window in black lace. She leaned out of the window and was telling the man just how much she charged, and she seemed to have a long list of prices.'

'Did he go in?' asked Johannes.

'No, he shrugged and went away, and she shouted something that must have been very rude as some of the people on the bank laughed and seemed to know what they said.'

'Is that all? It happens all the time,' said Johannes in a bored tone.

'Just an outlet for another appetite as simple as hunger,' whispered Kathy. 'No love, no real feeling, no tenderness, just . . . satisfaction, and you and Michiel take it for granted that most women are like that, ready to have sex with no love.' She sat quite still and gazed out of the window until the boat docked and the passengers left for their hotels. Elliot was tired and her professionalism came to her aid as she made sure he was comfortable, and Johannes gave him a sleeping pill before he ordered coffee to be sent up to the sitting-room. 'I'll drink coffee with you, Kathy, as I have to check with the clinic before I go to bed. Michiel might want to talk to me about his case, and I'd like to hear what he has done.' He glanced at Becky, who was closing the door of her room and could now hear everything they said. 'Damn!' he said softly. 'I can't talk now.'

'His case?' Kathy glanced at him and her voice was scathing.

'His case,' said Johannes firmly.

'Surely he won't be back yet?' she said.

'He said he wouldn't be long tonight,' said Johannes. He picked up his jacket and sighed. 'Don't lose any sleep over this, Kathy. You just don't understand, and I can't begin to explain now.' Becky was tidying magazines on the other side of the room, and the waiter brought in the tray of coffee-cups and a huge pot of steaming coffee. He set it down and added a plate of pastries to the tray before leaving, but by then Becky was back, examining the pastries with avid interest as if she had eaten nothing since breakfast.

'I saw what happened,' whispered Kathy. 'Nobody forced him to go there, and the girl obviously knew him.'

'You have to believe me. He didn't go there for sex,' Johannes said in a low voice.

Becky came over and handed him a cup and put the cream-jug within reach. 'It's very good coffee,' she said. 'Please take these cakes away, or I'll eat the lot and put on pounds.'

'I'll take them all with me,' said Johannes. 'I think Michiel will need something to sustain him tonight if he's coming with me to check the clinic.'

'You *are* expecting him?' Kathy said coldly. 'I would have thought that after a busy day he would want to sleep.'

'He can please himself.' Johannes was very brusque. 'What he does is his concern and no business of mine, or yours, or anyone's unless he makes it their business.' He brushed the crumbs from his jacket and stood up. 'Michiel is a very private person, a good doctor and, as you have met him only a few times, you can know nothing about the real man.'

Kathy drew away. Johannes suddenly reminded her of the censorious Customs officer, and his eyes held none of the warmth they had displayed earlier. Becky looked at him in amazement, and watched him leave with the pastries in a plastic bag he produced from his pocket. 'He might have waited for a chat,' she said. 'Elliot is out like a light, and we have at least two more hours before I want to go to sleep.'

'I'm going to write a letter,' said Kathy. 'I haven't even sent a picture postcard to anyone yet.' She forced a smile. 'I've eaten too much and drunk too much wine, and I think I'll write for a while and go to bed.'

Becky looked cross. 'I get so bored when Elliot goes to bed and leaves me to amuse myself. I can't go out alone or he'd be annoyed—he likes to know where I am.'

'Officially, you are his secretary, but he does take a lot for granted,' said Kathy. 'Perhaps you should please yourself and show him that you aren't tied to him, and that if he wants you for keeps he should make other arrangements.' She laughed. 'At least you wouldn't be left alone while he goes to bed.'

Kathy closed her bedroom door behind her firmly. 'I've seen enough of Holland,' she said to herself. 'Tomorrow, I'll telephone VSO and ask if they can give me an answer soon. I must get away.' She tried to shut out the scene she had witnessed by the canal, and knew that she was jealous of the girl in the blue gown, and would have given a lot to have Michiel Raynor look at her with such warmth . . . and affection.

She gave a wry smile. A white coat that could have fitted someone twice as large as she was, and smelling of noxious things, was no match for a filmy blue chiffon gown that drifted and clung, and most certainly the girl must have smelled like the perfume from the tiny bottle. Even if there was nothing between them, the contrast was obvious, and Kathy knew that she could not compete.

'Well, he shall have that back!' she said and sealed the bottle in a stiff brown envelope. She addressed it to Dr Michiel Raynor, but had no idea of Johannes' address. Perhaps I should address it to the girl in blue, second floor up and third house along the canal, she thought bitterly, and decided to leave the package in reception, as Michiel usually asked if there were messages for him when he came to visit Elliot, in case Elliot was out and wanted him to know when he'd be back.

She wrote to a couple of friends at Beattie's, and tried to make the letters amusing and relaxed, as she knew they envied her freedom to volunteer for work abroad. Her pride forbade any mention of Michiel Raynor and the havoc he was causing to her emotions after such a short time in Amsterdam. They knew about her affair with Tim, and Angela had said the things that many must have thought at the time—that his habits with women were well known to all but the women involved, and she was well rid of him.

Kathy gave a reluctant smile. Angela would be horrified if she knew that the calm and efficient girl who had surprised everyone by falling for Tim was now teetering on the edge of falling in love again. 'Maybe I'm just daft!' she murmured, and wrote about the museums. Women often fell for the same type twice. Patients married to drunks left them and remarried . . . drunks, or men with whatever other nasty habits the first man had. So maybe Michiel was unable to resist women, just as Tim had been.

But she gazed out of her window sadly and knew that he was not like Tim. He wasn't a womaniser. She *liked* Michiel, as well as being attracted to him, even when he was cross, whereas she had not really liked Tim when they had been apart and when she hadn't had the heady sensuality of physical contact to blind her to sensible thought.

She had forgotten to buy stamps, but knew that the receptionist might have some, so she walked quietly from the suite, hoping to avoid meeting Becky again that night, and went down the stairs rather than take the lift which was near to the door.

The foyer was deserted and she rang the bell for service. The girl handed her the stamps she required, and Kathy sat down to enclose a brochure of the hotel in each letter, knowing that the girls would be interested in where she was staying. She started as a soft, warm body rubbed against her shin, and saw a beautiful and very large cat that had something of a Persian in its family history, but also the rather predatory and knowing look of a Siamese. It purred loudly and jumped on to her lap with the complete confidence of one who recognises a cat-lover.

The girl behind the desk spoke sharply in Dutch and the cat bristled, but stayed where he was. 'It's all right,' said Kathy. 'I love cats.' She rubbed the glossy fur that made a deep ruff round the handsome face, and she laughed at the strange combination of genes that had produced this wonderful monster. 'You'd never win a prize for purity of breeding,' she told him, 'but you'd outdo any in the show for looks and sheer cheek.'

The cat stretched luxuriously and sheathed his claws as soon as she said no to his scratching her skirt. 'Handsome and cunning and willing to please if it suits you,' Kathy said, but from his reaction to the girl at the desk Kathy knew that he would be quite fierce and stubborn if crossed. Just like a typical handsome male of any breed, including man, she told herself.

'Don't settle down,' she said to him. 'I have to get to bed. It's been a rather trying day, I've had enough of handsome creatures, and you are shedding hairs all over my skirt.' She gently but firmly lifted him on to the chair at her side, and smoothed his head to show that there was no ill-feeling. He turned his head away to show his displeasure, but remained friendly, and then watched her walk towards the stairs.

'Kathy!' She stopped suddenly and wondered if she had imagined hearing Michiel's voice. 'Kathy,' he said again, and his hand caught her arm. 'I'm glad I found you. Did you have a nice day?' She glanced at him and then away quickly. His hair was slightly ruffled and he looked very attractive, with the air of success that a keen rugby player has after a hard and winning game. His eyes sparkled and he seemed not to notice her silence and the pallor of her face. 'I called in on the way back to Johannes' place and hoped you weren't in bed. I made an appointment for you to look over the big new hospital tomorrow, and I hope to meet you there during your visit. Here is a card with the names of people you might like to meet, and after that we can have a coffee and talk shop.'

'You haven't seen Johannes this evening?' she asked. He shook his head. 'He will tell you about this evening.

I'm very tired.' Michiel's smile faded. 'By the way, I packaged this for you as I have no use for it, and it must belong to one of your . . . friends.'

'Are you ill?' He swung her to face the light. 'You didn't prick your hand the other day? Tell me! I'd never forgive myself if anything like that happened to you.' There was agony in his eyes, his grip was urgent, and his anxiety was sweet torture as his eyes darkened and grew serious and he held her close, his lips questing over her hair and brow, but Kathy drew away from him.

'I'm fine. I took all reasonable precautions and have no fear of infection. I avoided contagion when I worked with infectious cases at Beattie's, and I have nursed some cases of VD, so I know what to do.'

'Something is wrong,' he insisted. 'You must be ill.'

'Nothing,' she said gently. Her hand went up and she touched the lock of hair that fell over his eyes, wanting to bring his face down to hers again and to forget any bad thoughts she had had. 'I am fine, and you don't know me well enough to have to concern yourself with me. I assure you that I am not sick. Just a fit of the blues. I shall enjoy the visit tomorrow, and thank you for arranging it. Please take this now, and return it to whom it belongs. It really is too potent for a girl like me.' She drew away, forbidding her hand to linger in that brief exquisite touch, but he reached out to take it, finding it as cold as he had imagined it must have been on the day he had first seen her waiting in the drizzling rain by a muddy field. She had been pale that day, while she had waited for another man, and she had disappeared after the match before he could speak to her and find out who she was. She had the same sad expression now, and he wondered if she was still in love with Tim Stone.

Kathy walked away up the stairs and didn't look back, and he didn't see the one large tear roll down her cheek, or the quivering lips, as he gazed after her, all humour and elation dying before he slowly walked to his car.

CHAPTER FIVE

LACK of sleep and her confused thoughts made Kathy pale and lacklustre when she appeared for breakfast. Time and again she had tried to forget much of what Johannes had said, and to believe that he and Michiel were not as cynical about real love as he had tried to make her believe. Not for a moment could she believe that Michiel had sex with a woman from the red-light district, but she recalled the expression of pleased recognition when he had looked up at the high window and then gone into the house of the girl in the pale blue gown.

'Bad night?' asked Becky. 'You should have stayed up and listened to the pop concert. I had it on my Walkman in bed, and it sent me to sleep when the music turned dreamy at the end.'

'The pancake I ate on the boat was a bit solid,' said Kathy. 'Too heavy for me at night.' She checked the tray with Elliot's breakfast on it, and took it in to him, trying to appear cheerful. 'It's a lovely day, Elliot. What are your plans?'

'Letters that can't wait, and then maybe one of the churches before lunch. I was tired last night, and by the look of you, I wasn't the only one. The boat was stuffy with all the windows shut and that awful woman at the next table wouldn't have one opened.'

'I'll do your routine morning check while you're at rest, Elliot,' Kathy said. 'Stay there until we've finished breakfast and cleared the room for your papers, and then take it easy this morning. I can get all the leaflets if you'll tell me which church we are to visit, and this afternoon I suggest that you rest again here. Becky will be with you, and I have been invited to look at the new hospital.'

Elliot shrugged. 'I don't know how a pretty girl like you can see all those terrible things.' He raised his hands in mock horror. 'What a way to fill precious leisure time. Go with my blessing, but don't bother to tell me all about it when you come back. That's what I like about Michiel. He never mentions his work unless I ask about it, and he has a fund of other topics that do interest me.'

'He's a very private person,' said Kathy. 'Or so Johannes told me. I know nothing about his private life.'

'Oh, not so private,' said Elliot. 'He has a very nice house in Wales, and is a keen yachtsman when he has time, but since his fiancée drowned while they were with a party on a boat in the Aegean, two years ago, he has been sailing very seldom and seems to think of nothing but his work. It wasn't the only tragedy in his life—his sister died of meningitis when she was small. I think that's why he decided to take up medicine.'

'He told you all this?' said Kathy, in wonder.

'No, he didn't mention it. You are right, he never discusses his affairs with anyone, but I have a friend who knew him when his own son was with him in medical school. There was a rumour that the girl whom he was to marry, and who was obsessed with him, took drugs and wasn't all she could have been in other respects. My friend said that it was a shock when Michiel announced that he wanted to marry her, and it was thought that he was just being Sir Galahad and hoped to reform her and wasn't really in love.'

'Perhaps he is attracted to women who are into vice,' said Kathy.

'What a thing to say!' Elliot looked disapproving, and put far too much butter on his toast. 'He isn't like that. Dedicated to his work, maybe, but not the kind to lust after saucy black underwear, and man enough to have a full life when he wants it, without having to look for comfort in dark corners.' He sighed. 'Go and have your own breakfast and tell Becky to bring in my briefcase at nine o'clock.'

'Half-past nine,' said Kathy. 'First I must take your blood pressure.'

'Get out of my sight, you big bully,' he said with a contented smile. 'I do love being spoiled.'

'What's so funny?' said Becky sharply when Kathy returned to the sitting-room.

'Elliot is in good form, and I think is beginning to feel that life can be lived, instead of being nibbled at cautiously round the edges in case something drops off!' Kathy laughed, and began to feel as if she, too, was likely to live as the sun shone and her natural enjoyment of life refused to be suppressed. She sat down and drank her fruit juice. The selection of food that made up the average Dutch breakfast never ceased to amaze her. There were four kinds of bread, each delicious and smelling fresh from the bakery, three neat arrangements of cheeses and fresh fruit, hard boiled eggs and thinly carved ham, and some fruit cake.

Becky sighed. 'This place does nothing for my weight. I can't resist these crispy rolls and I adore cheese. How do you keep so slim?' She watched Kathy help herself to ham and a boiled egg and toast.

'Protein instead of starch and sugar, and I worry a lot,' said Kathy with a smile. She felt better and, after a second cup of the good coffee that seemed to be a feature of Holland, as she had yet to drink a cup of bad coffee there, she was ready for the day, dismissing all the dark moments that had spoiled her sleep. I've come here to work and to enjoy a break, she told herself firmly, and I'll not let one man spoil it for me.

She even looked forward to her afternoon visit to the hospital, and reasoned that she had worked for a long time with men of all kinds, often very good-looking men, and could keep this visit on a professional level, but she would now be on her guard and not let feelings develop into more than a shared interest in work.

Elliot was in his dressing-gown when she went back to his room. Kathy took his blood pressure and noted his pulse and respiration rates. He was breathing well, but slightly faster than yesterday, and she made up her mind to observe his breathing when he didn't know that she was doing so. Often, in hospital, she had talked to a patient with asthma or other breathing problems, or someone awaiting an operation on the thyroid gland, and had tried to note the respiration rate before she produced a thermometer and the sphygmomanometer to do the other routine tests.

'You know yourself how you are seldom conscious of the way you breathe until it is brought to your notice, and then it comes in patchy bursts as if something is wrong,' her old sister-tutor had said, and Kathy found this to be true of patients, especially those of a nervous disposition.

'Is Becky ready for me?' he asked. 'I'll stay like this until we finish the letters, and then dress for the visit to the Oude Kerk. I have been there once and want to see the renovations they have made to the beautiful spire and leaning tower.' He glanced at his watch. 'The letters will take an hour at most, so can you fetch me at eleven? We might have time to see the Prinsenhof, if there's not too much to see in the church.'

'I have the details of that, too,' said Kathy. 'It was a convent before William the Silent lived there.'

'And died there, don't forget. Philip II of Spain paid an assassin to murder him, and he died at the foot of the winding staircase. The bullet holes are still there to prove it!' said Elliot with a gleeful relish that reminded Kathy of an eager schoolboy.

'I shall look forward to seeing it,' said Kathy, laughing. 'What a lovely morning we shall have, seeing scenes of ancient death and destruction!'

She sat by the window when Becky was absorbed in her shorthand notes and Elliot was dictating. His breathing had gone back to normal, and Kathy decided that he had anticipated that she would check his respirations and they had become uneven in the bedroom while he was aware of this.

Reassured, she left the suite quietly and wandered down to buy more picture postcards. Her earlier bad impression of Amsterdam was fading and she now welcomed the swish of the trams and the ever-pervading sounds of music from the old street organs that were a feature of the city. She walked and sometimes paused to look in shop windows, and it was nearly time to collect Elliot when she returned to the hotel, wishing that she could linger in the square and watch the vibrant young crowds, and maybe join a group of American and German tourists who were laughing and having a really good time, even if they couldn't afford the big hotels, and carried backpacks and sleeping-bags.

The elevator was open on the wrong floor, and she could hear the chatter of the room-maids who were changing linen in vacant bedrooms on the first floor, so she walked up the stairs and side-stepped a huge linen basket that had been left too near the stairs.

Kathy closed the lift door to make sure that Elliot wasn't faced with a walk downstairs, which might have been good for his health but not for his temper, and found him waiting for her. Becky was hard at work at the portable typewriter. 'You can tell the maids they can change the beds now,' Becky said. 'They tried to come in when we were busy, and I sent them away, but I think they are in the corridor now. Leave the door open and they'll know we are ready for them.' She sighed. 'I have a mountain of work to do, and more mail arrived this morning. It's as bad as being in a very busy office.'

'We'll go out to dinner tonight,' said Elliot. 'The sooner you get done, the sooner you can go window-shopping, but those letters must be sent today,' he added heartlessly, and Kathy stifled a smile, thinking how like an old married couple they were in every way but one.

The car was waiting and Elliot was in a very good mood. His knowledge of Amsterdam was impressive, and he was interesting company. Kathy found it hard to remember that he had been ill and must not overtax his strength until he had recovered completely. The few drugs that were necessary were being cut down each week, and it was only when she checked the bag she carried with her at all times, and into which she slipped the inhaler when he was with her, that she could imagine him needing the inhaler or any other treatment for asthma.

At one o'clock, Kathy insisted that they drag themselves away from the collection of silver and the relics of the House of Orange in the Prinsenhof museum, and went back for lunch. The car they had ordered was waiting, and she was surprised how the time had fled and how much she had enjoyed the whole morning.

Perhaps when she no longer saw or heard from Michiel she would forget him and be able to enjoy all the normal things that had filled her mind and life so pleasurably in the past. After all, she told herself, he was just a man she had met a few times. He was physically very attractive and virile, but so were other men, and it was strange how she could now think of Tim without a cold hand clutching her heart. All they had in common was their work. The frisson of dangerous magic was something she must guard against, as it could lead to nothing but a passionate and brief affair. Feelings stimulated by his nearness, stupid hopes that he might come to love her, and the sensation of loneliness when he was not there, must be dismissed, and other matters must fill her mind.

She carried the parcel of silver replicas bought at the museum shop, and left Elliot to check with reception that there was no more mail waiting for him.

She felt strong, and thought she would be able to meet Michiel in the atmosphere of white coats and sterile trolleys at the hospital in the afternoon. In that situation she thought she could face him without being affected by his physical charisma. She had been stupid and weak, imagining emotions that were unreal. What did it matter to her if he went into a house in the red-light district?

'Hello, Kathy.' Michiel came to meet her at the door of the suite, but did not touch the hand that she extended as if to ward off a blow. He gave a quizzical smile. 'I know I invited myself to lunch, but surely it isn't that much of a shock? Elliot did invite me, but I thought I might be too busy to take up the invitation.'

Becky had come through from the sitting-room into the tiny foyer of the suite. 'Perhaps she isn't sure if you are pure,' she said, laughing. 'After hearing about the other afternoon, I think we should avoid you as we don't know where you've been. Johannes made me feel sick when he told me about the clinic.' She laughed. 'I think we're safe, Kathy. He assures me that he hasn't been to the clinic yet.' She held up a pile of letters. 'I've been so industrious, and now I can get shot of these. See you in five minutes. Lunch is in the dining-room downstairs today. I'll take Elliot along if he's down there and save him another journey in that creaking lift.'

Kathy brushed past the man who stood in her path. 'Must leave my packages and wash my hands,' she said breathlessly.

'Kathy, wait! I saw Johannes and he seems to think that you have a very bad opinion of me, based on something you think you saw.'

'I don't know what you mean. What you do away from Elliot is none of my business, and of no real interest to me,' she said, and forced a smile. 'Thank you for arranging this afternoon. I shall enjoy it. Now please let me pass and get ready for lunch. Elliot hates women who keep him waiting.'

Michiel took her by the shoulders and shook her gently, but with a measure of irritation. 'Go and wash and I'll join Elliot and say that you are coming. Some time, you'll have to listen, Kathy, but it's a long story.'

He held her close for a second and she shut her eyes to hide her controlled pain. The feather-touch of his lips on her cheek made her shudder as she resisted the desire to turn her lips to his and to let her body mould against his firm thighs. He released her as if she had struck him, thinking that her reaction was revulsion, and he left the room as suddenly as he had appeared, leaving her to sway against the door and struggle to regain her composure.

Kathy had the memory of his mouth softly brushing her face and the sight of the over-bright tie he was once again wearing. Somehow, she knew that it meant he had made another visit to the house on the canal. It was a tie that he could have acquired anywhere, from a rack outside one of the cheap souvenir shops maybe, or from one of the music-loud boutiques in every high street in each modern city, but she was convinced that the girl in the lovely diaphanous blue gown had given it to him, and he had the nerve to flaunt it when he was with her. Doctors took off white coats when they left a ward. Surgeons never wore surgical boots away from the theatre, and even general practitioners didn't sit down to eat with their families wearing clothes that they had worn in infected houses, so why wear that tie now?

Quickly, she washed her hands and tidied her hair before stepping out into the corridor where Michiel lounged against the window-sill and looked down into the busy canal, where small boats now plied for hire and a canal-barge was edging along to a landing-stage beside another large hotel to collect people for a long afternoon trip. 'Ready?' he said without smiling.

'There was no need to wait,' she said.

'I wanted to make sure you came to lunch. I have to get to the hospital early to see a patient, and I'll hand you over to a friend who will show you the intensive care unit, and then I'll meet you in the children's ward.'

'If you are busy, I can come another day,' she said, almost willing him to postpone the outing. 'You do seem to have become involved with the sick during the short time you've been here, and it isn't fair to take up your time,' was her only other comment.

⊷ IT'S A ⊱
MILLS & BOON HONEYMOON
A SWEETHEART
OF A FREE OFFER!

FOURTEEN NEW MILLS & BOON ROMANCES—FREE!
Take a "Mills & Boon Honeymoon" with 14 exciting
Romances—yours FREE from Mills & Boon Reader Service.
Each of these novels brings you all the passion and tenderness
of today's greatest love stories . . . your free passports to bright
new worlds of love and foreign adventure!

But wait . . . there's <u>even more</u> to this great offer!

GLASS OYSTER DISH SET ABSOLUTELY FREE! You
will love these choice and delicate ornaments exquisitely
modelled to add a pretty touch to your sitting room, hall or
bedroom. Store precious little things in them or keep them
handy for sweets or nuts.

SPECIAL EXTRAS—FREE! You'll get our free monthly
newsletter packed with news on your favourite writers,
competitions, special subscriber offers, forthcoming books,
and much more.

FREE POSTAGE AND PACKING—There are no hidden
costs. Join Mills & Boon Reader Service and enjoy the
<u>convenience</u> of previewing 14 brand new Romances every
month, delivered right to your home before they're available
in the shops. Each book is yours for only £1.35 and with total
convenience this adds up to a sweetheart of a deal for <u>you</u>!

S̶TART YOUR MILLS & BOON HONEYMOON TODAY—
JUST COMPLETE, DETACH AND POST YOUR FREE OFFER CARD!

'It's not my first visit to Amsterdam,' he reminded her. 'Obviously I have contacts to follow up and friends to visit, but I can choose my own schedule and still have free time for you, Kathy. The medics at the hospital have been very good in allowing me to take in my own patients at times. The fact that I help Johannes, free of charge, gives me admission to many inner circles of care that I couldn't have as a visitor and onlooker at the hospital, and I do enjoy this place and want to share it with you.'

'Do you always stay with Johannes?' she asked.

'Not always.' He eyed her curiously. 'Something has gone wrong, Kathy,' he said quietly. 'I'd hoped to get to know you better. Perhaps you'll understand more after today.'

She walked quickly into the restaurant and towards the table where Elliot was examining the menu. Elliot looked up and made a face. 'Not that tie again! It's enough to ruin my appetite.' He laughed. 'At least I shan't see it this afternoon, and I pity the poor patients if they have to look at it when they are feeling less than well.' He chose vichyssoise soup and grilled fish, and Becky sighed and chose the same. She looked at Kathy's prawn salad without envy, except for Kathy's will-power in choosing something that would not put on an ounce of weight, and saw that Michiel was just as frugal, and seemed disinclined to eat even the small amount he had ordered.

'Before I forget,' said Elliot, after tasting his glass of dry white wine. 'You ordered a cab to take you both to the hospital after lunch, and the girl in reception asked if you'd mind giving a lift to a woman who has to visit there today. She's in a bit of a state, and doesn't know Amsterdam, and dreads walking into a strange hospital as she is afraid that no one will understand what she says.'

'Of course we don't mind,' said Kathy quickly.

'If she isn't ready by the time we want to leave, she'll have to order another taxi,' said Michel, frowning, but Kathy gave a mental sigh of relief. Another person in the close confines of the taxi would not allow any but the most general conversation, and she could avoid a confrontation with Michiel.

As if to try to be out of the hotel before the other woman joined them, Michiel looked at his watch and suggested that Kathy might leave coffee until they could drink some at the hospital. 'They are sure to offer us some there, and there's a limit to what anyone can drink in this city, as it's so strong and very black,' he said.

His smile was forced when he saw the woman waiting by the street door, her jacket over her arm and her handbag clutched as if she were a refugee. Kathy smiled at her, and tried to reassure her about the fact that it was true that most of the local people spoke a little English, and many spoke it well, with hardly a trace of accent.

Michiel said little as the taxi found short cuts and negotiated narrow canal-banks, over cobbled paths and the roots of trees that surfaced under the banks and lifted the cobbles. They passed small shops selling handicrafts from Indonesia and other former Dutch colonies, and Kathy wished that this could be just a carefree outing, to browse in such shops, and perhaps to buy small souvenirs to take back to England.

But soon I shall be working in countries where there are many ethnic crafts. I have no need as yet to buy souvenirs of foreign cities, or to fill my bags with things that will have to be given away or stored when I leave England for work with the Voluntary Services

Overseas, she remembered, and for the first time the prospect filled her with nothing but dread. No longer was it an escape. Where was the enthusiasm that had fired her to apply, and to have the patience to wait until she was called for duty, to serve somewhere exciting and new?

Michiel was gazing out of the window and she had time to study his face. The strength of his jaw boded ill for any who tried to take advantage of him. His mouth was generous and his nose was slightly out of true, as if it had been in close contact with a cricket ball or the sharp elbow of a tackling opponent, but the cleft in his chin was endearing, and she wondered if the women in his life had traced its outline and ended up by his lips.

He grinned and Kathy blushed, realising that he could see her intent inspection through the reflection in the slightly dusty glass of the taxi window. 'Yes, I did get a slight crack on the nose during a match against your hospital,' he said. 'A good excuse for making one of their star sisters work for me. I think that Beattie's owes that much to me.'

The other passenger looked confused. 'Who is Beatty?' she asked, and Kathy explained that it was the pet name given to her training hospital and the medical school that supplied the muscle for rough games on muddy fields.

'Nothing like this hospital. Here you will have very dedicated doctors, and nurses who will do exactly as they are told,' said Michiel with a laugh. 'At least, that's my ideal situation and the dream of every doctor, and one day I may find it.'

Kathy gazed up at the sleekly designed front of the enormous building. 'I'll come with you to ask where your nephew is warded,' she offered.

'No, I can see the man who will show you the

intensive care unit, Kathy. I will see that Mrs Marten is taken to the right ward. My Dutch happens to be that much better than something you learned overnight from a phrase-book!' Michiel insisted. 'Willem, this is Sister Tyler. Kathy, Dr Willem van Steen will take care of you. See you in Kids,' he added, and led Mrs Marten away as if it had been his idea to bring her, and he had never tried to leave her behind so that he could talk to Kathy alone in the taxi.

The next hour was so engrossing that Kathy forgot Michiel and her unease whenever he was near. The recovery rooms and intensive care units were modern and spacious. The busy staff were efficient, with the air of competent, unhurried expertise that marked a good working environment and a happy and hopeful place of recovery. Monitor screens flickered and drips took life-giving fluids into tired veins, and a hushed many-sounded background seemed not to disturb, but to give comfort to the sixteen patients, each enclosed in his bubble of efficiency and care.

'Time to move on,' Dr van Steen said at last. 'Michiel will have finished his visit and be ready to take over now in the children's department. Give my love to Marijke. Tell her the doctor with the toy duck will see her later.'

'Toy duck?' asked Kathy as soon as Michiel joined her. He was wearing a borrowed white coat and still flaunted the bright tie which was clearly visible. 'And who is Marijke?'

'Come and see. She is a child who came in with acute iritis, which was diagnosed in time to prevent any real lasting loss of sight, or so we hope. The cause hasn't been established, but it must have been a bad infection, and she was brought in by her mother who noticed that her eyes watered a lot and she couldn't bear bright

Michiel outlined the possible treatment. 'You know what to do?'

Kathy nodded. 'Every possible drug is ready. I check them each morning to make sure that a syringe is at hand in a special drawer which I keep locked,' she said.

'The last check showed his heart to be normal in function, so we shall have to risk giving him something much stronger than his antihistamine inhaler. I can't think why he should have an attack just now. He's relaxed, under good care, and has time to rest and to enjoy life. Did he do too much this morning?'

'No, he accused me of fussing because I wouldn't let him do more than the church and the small museum, with a rest for coffee half-way. He wasn't out of breath, even when we had to climb about thirty stairs, and he said he had never felt better.' She frowned. 'The mail came this morning, and the second post before we came away, so I know there were no shocks there. Elliot is wealthy, but he doesn't bite his nails if his shares drop a point or two and he isn't obsessed with business, although he is on the board of many companies.'

'Then it is something external and allergenic,' Michiel decided. 'It must be. Have you been putting more flowers in his room?'

'No! And it wasn't me who put the first lot in his bedroom,' Kathy reminded him. 'I've checked each day, and Becky has a vase in her room and green plants in the sitting-room, but no pollen-bearing flowers near Elliot.'

'Do you keep flowers in your room?' he asked, and his smile reached his eyes as if remembering something precious. 'You looked very beautiful, framed in carnations and freesias and looking very cross with me for accusing you of leaving the flowers in Elliot's room.'

His glance was eloquent and she looked away. Men who were susceptible to pretty women did notice such things, but it meant nothing.

'I love flowers,' she said, 'but I would never put a patient at risk in any way that I could avoid.' Her voice sounded stilted and cold, and she drew away from him to hide the fact that she was secretly touched that he had remembered. She had to convince herself that he said such things to any woman he fancied, in passing, and she would be in Amsterdam for a very short while.

'This may have at least one good result,' he said. 'I hope that Elliot isn't really ill, but he will need a nurse for far longer than we thought, and you couldn't leave him now, could you, dear little dedicated sister that you are?' His teasing laughter made her blush. 'VSO may have to wait,' he said.

He paid the cab driver and followed Kathy into the hotel, both hurrying. They ran up the stairs, as once again the elevator was open on the wrong floor. 'So, like it or not, you have to see me sometimes and you might as well accept me as I am,' he said, and thrust open the door to the suite, relieved that it had been left slightly open to admit them as soon as they arrived.

Elliot was propped up on a pile of pillows and his face was pinched with the effort needed to breathe out. Becky sat on the edge of the bed, holding his hand, and the usual mild inhaler lay on the small table.

'Stethoscope?' Michiel demanded, and Kathy thrust it into his hand before going to her room to open the bag of emergency drugs. Quickly, she unwrapped a new insufflator and cartridges of salbutamol, and loaded the insufflator, then took it to Michiel for immediate use.

'The dose is two hundred micrograms,' she said crisply. 'Is that enough at this stage?' Michiel nodded and Kathy gave him the insufflator and then drew up two hundred milligrams of hydrocortisone for the intravenous injection.

There were tears in Becky's eyes as she sat back, exhausted, and left the professionals to move in, gaining comfort from their practised care and confidence. The stifled breathing became easier, and colour flooded back into Elliot's cheeks.

'Better not give more just now,' said Michiel in a low voice. 'He's not reacting badly as far as his heart is concerned, but there is bound to be a degree of shock after the inhalation of such a strong substance.'

'Thank you,' said Elliot weakly. He gave a sweet smile to Becky, who was openly crying. 'I'm not going to die yet, you silly girl. Can't think what brought this on.'

Gradually, the wheezing stopped altogether and Kathy washed and discarded the syringe used for the injection.

'Not inflammatory, not stress,' said Michiel thoughtfully. 'So there must have been an external trigger like flowers or grass.' He grinned. 'You haven't got a horse in here, I hope?' He leaned forward and removed a short brown hair from Kathy's cream-coloured shirt-collar.

Kathy stared at it and then gasped and went back to the bedside quickly. 'Cat fur!' she said. 'Hold him forward so that I can take off his dressing-gown. It's covered in cat hairs!'

'What the hell are you doing?' Michiel said as she rushed out to the balcony and left the offending garment in the fresh air. 'There's no cat here! He must keep warm. I know it isn't really cold, but he needs a dressing-gown.'

'Where was your dressing-gown before you put it on,

Elliot?' asked Kathy. She looked in the wardrobe, pulled out a thick cardigan and helped Elliot put it on.

'I came in here to rest as you insisted, and decided that I was a little tired, so I stripped off to my underwear and put it on, before I got under the duvet. I know the duvet is non-allergenic as we insisted on that before we came here. If necessary, I travel with my own pillows, etc.'

'Where do you keep the dressing-gown?'

'I was a bit annoyed. It was a in a heap on the floor. Must have slipped off the chair where I had put it, folded ready for use. It was a bit creased, and I remember blaming the room-maids for putting the bed-linen on it and letting it slip to the floor when they changed the beds and took away the pillowcases and towels.'

Michiel came back from the balcony and shook his head. 'You are right. The dressing-gown is covered with cat hairs. How did it get in here?' he said. 'The management know that you must never have cats near you, and yet, as Kathy noticed, the dressing-gown is covered in long cat hairs as if he made a bed of it while you were out this morning.'

'There is a huge cat in the hotel,' said Kathy. 'It was in the foyer one evening, and it is obviously free to walk anywhere. When the maids did the rooms, the outer door was open and he must have slipped in. The maids wouldn't think it odd if he appeared in a room, and he could have got away from the balcony as it is only a small cat-leap from one balcony to the next in this hotel.'

'I'll send the gown to be cleaned,' said Becky. 'Meanwhile, you must sleep in my room while this is thoroughly cleaned, and I shall have another room somewhere.'

'No, Elliot will need you, Becky. I'll change my room

and you can ring through if you need me. I think that this is a one-off attack, and by this evening Michiel will be able to judge if there will be a recurrence.'

'Thank you, Kathy. You're right. I need Becky more than I need a nurse, unless I am ill, and I am not going to be ill again. Already, I can feel the difference now that the cat hairs have gone,' said Elliot.

'Your usual inhaler would have been enough if the cat hairs had not been so close to you all the time,' said Michiel. 'Now, will you think about the desensitisation programme I tried to persuade you to have in London?' He bent down to hear what Elliot whispered and laughed. 'I think you should,' he said. 'Have the course first, and then I'll be the first to congratulate you.'

Kathy smiled wistfully. Michiel was right that one good thing might emerge from this attack, but it wasn't to be an extension of her duties with Elliot. Just a marriage between her patient and his secretary, and Kathy would be free to go away. Free? Would she ever be free? She looked at the hands that had tended Elliot so carefully and with such tenderness, and knew that she would never forget their magical strength and gentleness.

She dared not recall the touch of his lips on hers and the fleeting agony of wanting that it brought her.

She saw the pleasure in the dark eyes as Michiel nodded his approval of Elliot's improved condition. They don't need me here now, she decided. I can go away and be forgotten. Michiel was laughing and bending over his patient. Once again she felt excluded, and knew that, for her, life would never glow again as once it had done in the carefree days at Beattie's during her training, before she had met first Tim, and now this enigmatic, wonderful, charismatic man, who confused her thoughts and emotions.

CHAPTER SIX

'SO, you are not far away,' said Michiel. 'The room next door to the suite, in fact, and the least that the management could do for you. I hinted that Sir Elliot might sue them for negligence, as they were fully aware of his needs and allowed him to be ill because they couldn't control their wretched cat.'

'Thank you for making all the arrangements,' said Kathy. 'Elliot enjoyed all the fuss, and after he recovered he sat on the balcony in a brand new silk dressing-gown doing a very good imitation of Noël Coward.' She was lost for words and found it difficult to talk to Michiel as a new shyness made her breath uneven and her voice tremulous, and she knew that she was blushing.

For a couple of hours they had worked together, and an undercurrent of warm understanding had made this time precious, as happened so often in hospital when a team had worked so hard all night to save a life. But now they were alone, and he was saying all the conventional things that he might say in the office of a ward sister after a ward round. She wondered if she had imagined the sensation of closeness and the frisson of sensuality that had sparked between them when they had made physical contact over the sick man's bed. He hesitated and then followed her into her room.

The sunlight filtered through the pale blue net curtains that covered the tall windows leading to the balcony, and the carpet was thick and luxurious, and so new that the pastel-coloured flowers in the design looked almost three-dimensional and ready to pick up from the floor. 'You can enjoy fitted carpets, but Elliot is better with cotton rugs and older carpets that don't throw fluff,' he said.

'You make it sound as if he is living in squalor,' said Kathy drily. 'I would hardly think that washed Chinese silk rugs and old Kashmir carpet squares are in that category.'

'Well, it was once used for the President of France when he stayed here years ago, and they still call it the Presidential Suite, and keep the good carpets, but this room is very comfortable and I shall enjoy sharing a night-cap with you here after dinner.' He glanced at her quizzically and she lowered her gaze before the challenge she saw in his eyes. He *had* been aware of her and the softening of her attitude towards him when Elliot had been so ill. The lightning sparks that his touch had transmitted had not been a one-way sensation, and Kathy knew that he was elated and confident and sure of her response. With a sense of panic, she wondered if he was assessing how far she would go in a more intimate relationship and if, as she suspected, he shared Johannes' opinon that sex was just something pleasant to satisfy a passing need.

He seemed relaxed, his dark hair was ruffled, and the deep brown eyes glowed with a dangerous warmth; it wasn't easy to retain her apparently cool manner. She tried not to watch his hands. They were not the hands of the fictional surgeon, with long, white, sensitive fingers. These hands were strong and gentle, with workmanlike fingers and immaculate fingernails, never restless, but eloquent when he talked, one finger jabbing at the air to stress a point of fact, and she wanted those hands to touch her, to take her close and to caress her hair.

'I shall stay in the sitting-room of the suite until I am sure that Elliot is asleep and doesn't need anything,' she said hastily. 'I have a key to the suite and the phone by my bed so that he or Becky can be in touch quickly if they want me at any time, and tomorrow the room will be cleaned and aired and he can move back—and so can I, as I feel responsible for him and ought to be on call.'

She avoided looking at Michiel, but suspected that he was laughing at her as if she were a prudish schoolgirl afraid to be alone with any man under eighty, but how could she relax enough to flirt with him as she might with any other man? A part of her longed to let her smile and indulge in the kind of banter that was normal between a man and a woman who found each other attractive, but knew that there would be a limit to that attraction, as it held no promise of commitment.

Kissing could be fun, she thought wistfully. A dimple appeared at one corner of her mouth as she stifled a sudden giggle. The poor man might be thinking of what he wanted for lunch, and not that her lips were soft and ready for love. She looked away. So much could be fun with Michiel if she accepted that it was just a brief encounter.

'What's funny?' he asked, and his smile was ready to share anything she liked to tell him.

'I was thinking about Elliot when I stripped off his dressing-gown. Outrage and a growing suspicion that he had a madwoman as a nurse!' she lied.

She had flirted with other men and had been intensely attracted to Tim, but this was different. This could be quite different. Heavy petting that stopped short of the whole act of love would never be enough between them, and so it must not happen unless a miracle made him want her forever.

'You don't look so fraught now,' he said.

'Fraught? I suppose we all did, and now it's a relief and I can smile again,' she said.

'That's not what I mean. When I saw you first, on that muddy field, you looked so unhappy.'

'I was frozen,' she said, and wondered just how closely he had watched her after the game when she had been waiting for Tim and had had to leave without him. He remembered me, she thought with amazement.

'No, don't clam up again, Kathy. I hoped that you were learning to relax, and maybe forget what it was that troubled you so much.'

'You know all about it, don't you?' Her voice shook, but she faced him with a pathetic attempt at defiance. 'I suppose it was laughed at by everyone who heard that Tim had been two-timing me for ages, and was well known for it. They say that the person most involved is always the last to know.'

'Nobody laughed,' he said. 'Not many people knew that you were going out together seriously, especially as he did take other girls out and you had many friends of both sexes.'

'But you knew! And I didn't know that you existed.'

'No, we didn't meet on the wards or at the many parties,' he agreed. 'I wasn't in your medical school, and came only by invitation and to play rugby, but I do have good friends at Beattie's, and I asked about you.'

'Why me?' She lifted an unsteady hand to her hair and pushed it back from her face. 'I feel as if you've spied on me, and wonder just what you saw.'

'I hate to see anyone unhappy, and if someone is beautiful and very good at her job, then it gives my concern an extra depth. I hate waste—of talent, beauty, and of life,' he said, and she saw that he wasn't joking.

In fact, his mouth had set as if his memories were bitter.

'I'm not wasting my life,' she said, and her eyes flashed with uneasy anger. Just what did he know about her? She shivered as if her body was stripped as surely as her mind had been under his unseen scrutiny, but the anger was tinged with pleasure that he had seen her, taken notice, and cared that she had been unhappy.

'Why did you run away, Kathy? I heard that you were in line for a senior job in Theatre.'

'I didn't run away. I wanted a fresh start away from Beattie's, and a job that would take all my talents, such as they are, and I hope to hear where I'm to be sent soon.' She saw his mouth widen into a smile and thought he was laughing at her again. 'What about you? Are you so different? You heal the sick and take time to come over to Amsterdam to work among the underprivileged and the children from the red-light district.' She tried not to think of the woman in the upper room and his real pleasure when he had seen her at her window and gone into the house.

The pale blue curtains billowed in the breeze as Michiel opened the doors leading to the balcony more widely, so that they could walk out and admire the view of the Amstel. A fold of the curtain touched her face as Kathy passed through the gap in the filmy material.

That was one reason why she could never let Michiel touch her now. Pale blue chiffon, or whatever the material that the woman had worn, had been so like this curtain, soft and yielding and delicately lovely, and yet it was a barrier as cold and hard as steel between her and the man who now seemed as pleased with his success over Elliot's recovery as a boy might be on being given a new toy spaceship. It wasn't possible that he had slept with her, but the easy acceptance of sex as a pastime had certainly influenced Johannes, so why not Michiel?

He turned to her as they stood looking across the Amstel, where once tall masts and full sails had filled the skyline, and sailors had shouted of victories on the high seas before coming in to port and unloading the treasure snatched from the Spanish and British merchantmen in the seventeenth century. She felt his arms round her and she trembled, and braced herself to resist, but his touch was gentle.

Instinctively, and forgetting her resolution, she let her face be lifted to his kiss, and closed her eyes.

'Thank you for your help,' he said. 'Elliot could have been really ill if you hadn't noticed the cat hairs on his gown.' For a second, Kathy felt that he wanted to kiss her more urgently, to hold her even closer and to let his desire rob him of control, then he kissed her again, even more softly, but with a lingering insistence that was more seductive than an onslaught of desire. It made her want to cling to him, shutting out the pale blue curtains and the conviction that he wanted her for casual amusement.

He looked down into her face. 'I have to tell you about Marijke,' he said. 'I have to tell you a lot of things, Kathy. She is one of Johannes' patients, and so is her mother. I became involved with them the last time I was in Amsterdam when Johannes was away in Leiden on a course, and as I knew something about eyes he asked me to come back and see what progress had been made in Marijke's condition. Helena was nearly frantic over the child, and full of guilt as she suspected that the infection came from somewhere close to home. So, we had a hysterical mother and a very sick child on our hands, living in unsuitable accommodation.'

Kathy shrugged away from him and leaned against the balcony rail, hoping that it would seem casual and not because she needed support. 'Where?' she asked, but she already knew. 'Does that child come from the home of a prostitute?'

'Don't sound so damned holy!' he said, and his sudden flush could have been anger or embarrassment. 'Helena isn't a bad woman. She's a good mother, and is giving up the life to marry a man she trusts,' he said defensively. 'She was driven to that life when she was deserted by a man and was pregnant for a second time, and Marijke was only three. She lost the baby and became dependent on prescription drugs. Johannes has got her off those, and she is truly overwhelmingly grateful to us both.'

'So you visit her in her room by the canal?' Kathy drew away, aware that Michiel was now smiling.

'Of course. I visit all my patients,' he replied.

'Patients who are so grateful, they usually want to give something in return?' Kathy suggested.

He laughed. 'She gave me this tie when I said I wanted something bright to make Marijke tell me what colours she could see, and little Marijke rifled her mother's handbag and gave me the perfume that you were so rude about,' he said.

'I hope you returned it,' she said in a flat voice. 'Surely it is a tool of her trade?' Kathy couldn't keep the bitterness from her voice.

'No.' He stared at her for a moment, and then drew away. 'It was given with love and gratitude, and I never insult a lady who has good intentions. I seldom insult any woman unless her manner is intolerable, and . . . intolerant,' he said in a soft voice that was as cold as ice. 'Intolerance when you know nothing of the circumstances is indefensible, and not very intelligent, especially in a nurse or doctor,' he added. 'And if you are thinking that I am mad enough to receive favours from Helena in return for my medical expertise, then you can believe what you like, and go to hell! She is a very beautiful woman, who is trying to make a new life for Marijke.'

His face lost all gentleness and his eyes were hard. He followed her back into the room and shut the windows so abruptly that the curtains billowed over Kathy's head in a veil, and she had to claw herself free, almost panic-stricken as if she were being stifled in pale blue gossamer.

'I'm sorry,' she said in a low voice, 'I didn't mean that. I'm sure you never could . . .' but the room was empty and it was too late to make him understand that she didn't believe it. Listlessly, she threw a dress on the bed and wondered if she could bear to wear blue ever again. She put the dress back on the hanger, and chose a sleekly fitting silk sheath of deep rose-pink that had a hint of a cheongsam in its style. That was no better. It had a slit skirt that revealed her leg almost to the thigh and was strictly for parties, and even then Elliot might find that too attractive and make Becky jealous. Finally she put on a simple white shirt tucked into a bright green and blue skirt, and piled on four necklaces of varying shades of green, one of which had a pendant of tiny pearls that were fake but very pretty, though not dramatic enough to be worn alone.

Elliot rang through on the house phone. 'Just testing,' he said. 'I feel half-dressed with you away from the suite, but come in as soon as you can. Michiel has allowed me to sit up for dinner here, and then he's taking you to see Johannes, I believe.'

'That was the arrangement, but now you aren't well we can't do that and leave you,' Kathy said. By now, she was sure that Michiel would regret the arrangement as much as she did, and Elliot was the perfect excuse for both of them not being away from the hotel at the same time.

'Rubbish. I'll have to get used to doing without you soon, as Becky pointed out, and now that I know I shall be fine after the desensitisation programme, which I now agree is necessary, I think I shall marry the girl.' He sighed. 'The sight of her tearful little face when I was ill convinced me that I must not lose her, so I suppose I must take the plunge.'

'Does she know yet?'

'Goodness, no! And don't you tell her. I need a lot more work done before I have to endure a new secretary.'

'You are a rogue, Elliot!' said Kathy, and felt better. 'I'll come in as soon as I'm ready.'

'Johannes rang,' said Rebecca when Kathy opened the door to the sitting-room. 'Michiel had a call to see a friend while he is in Amsterdam, and as his time here is limited Johannes will take his place, and is taking you to a jazz concert and to see the floodlit bridges from the Herengracht, wherever that may be. I hope you like traditional jazz,' she added with a malicious little smile.

'Great!' said Kathy with more enthusiasm than she felt. 'I think I prefer to go with Johannes, as he knows the city far better than anyone I've met.'

Becky looked disappointed. 'I thought you liked Michiel and would find Johannes a poor substitute.'

'Doctors and nurses can work together and enjoy it, but personal relationships are quite different,' Kathy said firmly. 'I am sure that Michiel has other interests here, and I have no intention of mixing work with pleasure as far as he is concerned.'

Dinner was a quiet time that gave Kathy room for

thought, as Elliot ate little and was tired after his acute attack during the day. As soon as he pushed aside his glass dish and left the half-eaten ice-cream gateau, Kathy suggested that it was time for bed, and he made no comment, but walked slowly to the bathroom to get ready for the night.

'I'll read to him a little, and then I have a new paperback that I want to get into this evening,' said Becky. 'Johannes has a car phone and can check with me later after the concert and decide if you can stay out later, and I have the number of the hospital. They will pass on a message to Michiel if he is required.'

'Do you know where that might be, in case we want to pick him up on the way back?' asked Kathy. She was curious to know if he was visiting Helena again, and was annoyed with herself for feeling jealous. She would have to forget him soon, and if Helena was a patient why think of her as any different from a hundred other women in a clinic? Unless . . . unless I'm jealous of such women who can take a man and make him happy with no inhibitions, no guilt, and with humour, she wondered, trying to be fair.

'He didn't say. He might be in one of two places, and the hospital will pass on a message wherever he is at a certain time,' said Rebecca. She shrugged. 'He said they would do it as a favour, as he isn't on their staff. They hinted that he can't expect them to act as a kind of telephone exchange for him, but they make a concession when he is dealing with Johannes' patients.'

I just hope that Johannes doesn't take me past that house again tonight, Kathy thought. She dropped the key to the suite into her bag, as now the management had give extra keys to her and to Michiel. The door was firmly shut at all times between the suite and the outer corridor to stop the cat from entering, and there was a large wooden screen at each side of Elliot's balcony, to stop anything coming from another balcony.

Johannes was dressed casually and eyed her with approval, as if she had dressed especially for his benefit. He noticed the smart flat shoes and grinned. 'Thank heaven for sensible girls who aren't likely to complain if I take them walking over rough ground in the dark,' he said. 'Michiel hopes to join us later, but first, if you can bear it, we visit Marijke. I wasn't sure how long you have left in Amsterdam, and I promised that you would come to visit her again. She took a great liking to you when she saw you. She did see you,' he added with satisfaction. 'Michiel asked her to describe you to him, and he said that she must have been able to see you fairly clearly to have been able to tell him so many details.'

'So you think she will regain most of her sight?' Kathy warmed to the man who looked so tough and yet cared so deeply about people in real need.

'There will be a slight loss, but she will lead a normal life once she is out of that house and into the country.' His voice took a cynical note. 'I shall believe that her mother has given up her work when it happens,' he said. 'It won't be easy to change her whole existence, even with a man who obviously loves her very much.' He gave a short laugh. 'It had better work. I introduced them, but I have my doubts, as he is an intelligent man with so much going for him.'

'Why have doubts?' she asked.

'I like women, and when I told her that the medication was working and that Marijke would not go blind, she offered to take me to bed as if she was offering me a cup of coffee! I never play around with my patients, and even if Michiel believes in her eventual separation from a cathouse, I can't quite beleive it. Women who are weak in one way are often weak in another, although I admit she came off drugs very well, and swears that she will give up her work as soon as Marijke is out of hospital and they have furnished the small house in the polders.'

'You refused her offer even when it was offered with gratitude and . . . love?'

'Four years ago I might have gone with her, when I thought I was able to take what I wanted from life and have no comebacks. Like everyone I knew as a student, I thought I was immortal! But I have seen too much disease since then to make me want to do that. No doctor in his right mind would go to bed with her. She finds Michiel and me quite odd in that way, and must think we are less than virile! I keep clear, and woo instead of buying.' He took her hand. 'I'm open to offers,' he added and laughed. 'No! Don't say anything. I know you wouldn't. Michiel thinks you some sort of nun who is afraid of the real world, and we don't sully nuns in Amsterdam.'

'Michiel thinks of me only as a nurse,' said Kathy. She blushed, knowing that this was a lie. Her reluctant reaction to his kiss had been enough to tell him that she had a warm and responsive heart, even if all her logic told her that he was not for her.

Johannes opened the door of a battered 2CV and Kathy laughed. 'Cinderella's coach,' said Johannes.

'I can imagine rats as footmen, but no Prince Charming,' she replied. 'Where did you get it?'

'I paid little, but it works,' he said. 'I am not risking my other car on these roads, and when it is parked and the cyclists rub against it with metal indicators scratching the sides, I do not, as you say, throw a fit, but I miss my car phone when I am in this heap.' He started the engine, which coughed and spluttered and finally agreed to start. 'Nobody steals it, and it drinks very little petrol,' he added with pride. 'But as we have no phone, remind me to check with Elliot for you later.'

'I can believe that no one would want it,' said Kathy, hanging on as they negotiated a bend and she bounced on the hard seat. 'If we are to see Marijke, I should take her a present.'

'No need. Sweets are banned and she has toys enough,' he said. 'Besides, the toy shops are closed and she will be too sleepy to notice anything but the fact that we came to see her. She may even be asleep, and our journey in my luxury carriage will be wasted.'

'Not wasted,' said Kathy as she climbed out of the car. 'A journey that I shall remember for a long time. It made a very great impression on me,' she said, rubbing her seat and laughing.

The hospital was throbbing with hidden energy. All the wonders of heating and cooling systems worked behind the high gloss of the walls and tiles, and the soft hiss of elevator doors had none of the swish and clang of the old doors in the lifts back in the older parts of the Princess Beatrice Hospital in London. It was efficient and impersonal, and the few members of staff who passed them in the long corridors were quiet and intent on where they were going. Kathy contrasted this place with the graffiti-covered walls of the clinic, and the smell of its kitchen with the odour of cleanliness in this hospital.

'It is good?'

Kathy smiled. 'Quite amazing. A bit different from the place where I was made to work the other day,' she added.

'The other place is necessary. Have you ever gone into a shop and fitted on clothes and seen your own trousers hanging up beside the smart new ones? I am always ashamed of the shabbiness of my own things, even if I felt good in them out in the street. People who have so little hate this place, as they sense that they are inferior and feel more comfortable in a house that matches their own shabby mode of dress and living.' Johannes looked at her seriously. 'Bright tiles and paint don't make good surgery or care. Care is people,' he said simply. 'Michiel is one of us, helping and not counting the hours, and never judging anyone by his clothes or circumstances.'

It sounded like a rebuke, and Kathy knew that she had been discussed. 'You both love your work, as I do mine. We may not agree on some things, but we are all working for people,' she said seriously.

He grinned. 'Don't look so solemn. Now, I *can* imagine you in uniform. Are you still intent on nursing brown babies?'

'Wherever they send me,' she replied, but the prospect didn't fill her with anticipation any more, and the future after she had to leave Amsterdam was an empty black hole that must be filled with the unknown that was no longer an adventure.

'Work here and help me,' said Johannes. She shook her head. 'Michiel will be leaving us next week, and I could do with an English-speaking sister to deal with the sick tourists. Some of the student types come and get high on drugs they can't handle, now that we are not seriously concerned about cannabis but are concentrating on hard-drug abuse.'

The ward door was open and the lights over the beds of the children were softly shaded to throw a muted light on to the beds, but not to disturb the sleeping children. A nurse bent over a child in a cot who was whimpering and restless, and other children snored gently or snuffled into the bedclothes. Marijke was

awake, and her eyes were dark and very bright as the
pupils were wide with the relaxing atropine drops. The
great beauties of past society had had eyes as bright and
fathomless when they had used the same plant as an
aid to loveliness, but here it was used for a more
rewarding medical purpose.

The child held out her arms to Johannes and smiled.
She spoke to him in her own language and he replied,
while Kathy sat and smiled, having no idea of what was
said. 'Come closer,' said Johannes. 'She wishes to see
you clearly and to touch the pretty necklaces.'

Kathy sat close to the bed and held the tiny hand.
Marijke stroked Kathy's wrist and gazed up at her with
complete trust. Kathy bent over the bed and her
necklaces swung away from her breasts. Marijke
touched the chains as if they were mobiles hanging over
a cot; the gold and enamel glowed green and blue, and
the small pearl pendant hung away from the rest.

'You have a way with children,' said a voice she knew
and which now made her start suddenly. Michiel stood
between her and the lights from the central lamps, and
seemed to loom as a shadowy cloak that might envelop
her and make her helpless. She felt stifled, as if this was
already happening, but couldn't move away. She found
that she was a prisoner in another way. Tiny hands were
now clutching the chain on which the pearls swung as
Marijke tried to see them more clearly in the soft light.
Fingers that she remembered for their medical expertise,
but which she now dreaded touching in case she wanted
to hold them against her lips, disentangled the chains
and unhooked the clasp of the pendant, telling the child
to loosen her grip, first in English as if he had forgotten,
and then in Dutch.

'She's going to waste it all on the Third World,' said
Johannes, laughing. 'I offered to let her stay here with

me, but she refuses.'

'She should stay and have children of her own,' Michiel said quietly, then laughed as if he was joking. He held the chain aloft, making the pendant move from side to side above the child's head.

Kathy took it from him and slipped the chain round Marijke's neck. 'She is getting too excited. The staff will be very cross if we don't leave. You both know better than to keep a patient awake long after she should be asleep.' The tenderness that Marijke had brought to her eyes lingered as she looked at Michiel.

'Yes, Sister Tyler,' said Michiel with a grin, as if he had completely forgotten that he had left her so hurriedly in the room overlooking the Amstel.

Marijke looked forlorn but sleepy as Johannes ruffled her hair and said goodnight. Michiel squeezed one small hand and stood away from the bed, but Kathy asked him to tell Marijke to keep the necklace and to remember the English Kathy. Gently, she smiled and kissed the child on one cheek, and Marijke gave her a sweet smile of thanks.

'That was generous,' said Michiel. 'She has had so little in her young life.'

'But her locker was loaded with toys,' said Kathy. 'She has more than most in that ward.'

'Not the necklace, although that was a generous gesture, if it meant anything to you. I mean the kiss. That was much more important. She will remember you, Sister Kathy.' His voice was almost sad. 'You will not see her again?'

'I doubt it,' Kathy said, trying to sound disinterested. 'And I believe that you, too, are leaving Amsterdam soon.'

'Not for the Third World,' Michiel replied. 'I shall be only a short flight away from Holland.'

'So you may come back?'

'Oh, yes, he'll be back,' said Johannes. 'Michiel does more than he admits. Foreign doctors are not always so welcome, but Michiel has a foot in both camps, and his Dutch ancestors now make him acceptable here, as well as his special knowledge.' He glanced at Michiel with affection. 'He's not one to forget old friends. And talking of friends, Kathy, join my exclusive club. I count you as one.'

They came to the old car. 'I'm not driving in that death-trap,' said Michiel firmly. 'I'll telephone the hotel to make sure that all is well, and we'll walk to the jazz concert. My car might attract graffiti or worse, but while that one is more in keeping with the Jordaan area, it's not fit for anything but the scrap-yard.'

'Please yourself,' said Johannes. 'I'll collect it tomorrow.'

'Be careful of that guy,' said Michiel as he turned to find a telephone. 'If he says he is your friend, be ready to be asked to do something you would never want to do if you hadn't been conned by him. See how I got involved in a city that has quite enough of its own medics!'

'I can't think what he means,' said Johannes with an air of injured innocence.

'Ask me,' said Kathy.

'If you insist!' he said, laughing. 'You have a flat in London?'

'I share a flat with another nursing sister,' Kathy agreed cautiously.

'A spare bed somewhere?'

'Mine while I'm away, but only floor space for a sleeping-bag when we are both there,' she said. 'Two small rooms and one sitting-room, and I shall be there soon, so my bed will be used.' She smiled. 'You can have the floor if you can't get all of your great hulk on to our rather narrow settee. When do you want it? I'd better warn Julia, as any girl with a nervous disposition would scream if she woke one morning and found a Dutch rugby half-back sleeping on the floor.'

'I shall be in London in a few weeks' time. May I phone the girl in the flat and say I am coming on your invitation?'

'Yes, you do that, and I'll send her a note about it. It's better to ring between nine in the morning and about seven at night, as she does mostly a late shift and sleeps during the day.'

'Elliot is asleep and fine,' said Michiel who came across the road to join them. 'Now what has this Dutch pirate asked you to do?'

'He just wants to shelter for a night or so in London. I can offer him a lumpy couch or the floor in my shared flat, but surely you have a bigger place somewhere that he could borrow?' Vaguely, Kathy recalled someone saying that Michiel had a house in Wales and other accommodation, but she couldn't be sure about this.

'Not at present,' said Michiel. 'I am between selling one apartment and buying another, so I, too, have to beg a resting place when I come to London. I share with a friend at Tommie's, but in all hospital hostels space is at a premium, and sometimes I have to use a hotel, now that I am not on the hospital staff until I take up a job on the staff, later.'

'Well, don't come together,' Kathy said. 'And Johannes has made the first bid for our floor.' She took out her diary, but the street-light was too dim to read anything and to see when Julia would be there.

'We'll have coffee in one of the Brown Cafés and you can make some kind of date for this visit, and give me your address, too,' said Michiel.

Kathy glanced at him. He was being very polite, and she didn't quite trust him in this mood. She waited until the huge bistro cups of steaming coffee were set before them, and then turned to her diary. 'I shall be back in London two weeks from today,' she said. 'Unless Elliot is ill again, he will return in about a month, and I hope to see them in London—unless I have left for Timbuktu, or somewhere equally strange. I shall continue to work for an agency until I leave, so I may be in London or anywhere they send me when you want to come to England,' she added. 'I'll lend you a key, Johannes, and if you come you can leave it with Julia when you have finished with it, but let us know when to expect you.'

She saw that both men made a note of what she said, and she had an uneasy feeling that Michiel thought that he might be included in the invitation almost as if he had more right to be with her than Johannes did. At least he hadn't asked for a key, and she couldn't oblige as she had only one spare key in her bag.

'Come on, they'll have started,' said Johannes. 'Jazz is international, and there'll be people from every country in Europe there tonight. It should be good. I always enjoy it better with a pretty girl at my side.' He draped an arm across Kathy's shoulders, possessively, and led her away as if they were together and Michiel was with them as an afterthought.

CHAPTER SEVEN

'WELL, that settles it! You'll never shift all those bicycles to reach your car now.' Michiel laughed. 'Go back to the concert. You know you didn't really want to leave, and I'll make sure that Kathy gets back to her hotel.'

'I'm sorry that either of you think I need an escort,' Kathy said. She smiled and her eyes were dreamy. 'It's the best concert I've been to in a long time, and I'd almost forgotten that I like jazz so much. Promise to tell me what they play in the bits I'm going to miss, Johannes.' She reached up and kissed his cheek. 'Any time you want a spare seat filled and I'm available, look no further!'

'You don't have to ask,' said Johannes. 'I wish you could stay. Why can't this great Philistine go back and do your night check on Elliot and leave us to wallow in the music?'

'And leave you to bring her back in that heap of a wreckage?' said Michiel scathingly, but with a touch of real annoyance.

'No way,' said Johannes. He put a hand over his heart. 'I would walk her home by the water and whisper in her ear that Dutch doctors are the best, the sexiest and the most interesting men in the world.'

'In that case, I go back with Michiel,' said Kathy, but her eyes sparkled. 'I feel really relaxed,' she added. 'Thanks, Johannes. I might even like the Dutch after tonight!'

'Come on, we'd better see what Elliot is doing,' said

Michiel.

Kathy sensed that he was not pleased. 'There's no need for you come all that way just to be told he's asleep,' she said. 'I can get a taxi, if that's possible just now, and if you give me a telephone number I'll ring as soon as I've been in to check. I'd hoped to slip away and catch a tram, like all those people waiting over there, but I suppose a taxi would be safer and quicker.'

'I'll go with you,' said Michiel in a voice that brooked no argument. 'I agree that you must go back now as you are his nurse, but I want to see him for myself. We can both be satisfied that he is all right, and then we can all have a good night.'

'OK,' said Johannes. 'I admit I'd like to go back. It's the first time I've really felt able to forget a lot of things, and it is a very good concert. I've been bushed for weeks, and almost unable to keep my eyes open for an emergency, but you've made all the difference, Michiel, and when Hans Arnhem comes back I can lead a fairly normal life again. I can even get out my little black book and date a few friends.' He winked at Michiel. 'Come here!' he said to Kathy, and enveloped her in a bearlike hug. 'A real flesh and blood woman, with absolutely nothing wrong with her!' He kissed her on the lips. 'I'll take you to see a windmill or two before you go back, and don't forget, we have a date in London.' He grinned. 'Maybe I can persuade you to stay here.'

'Maybe you can't,' said Kathy. 'Don't lose the key I gave you, and if I'm not in India or Africa I'll meet you under the clock at Piccadilly!' She was smiling.

'The music has started again,' said Michiel. Firmly, he led Kathy away, and Johannes loped along the path back to the concert.

'The taxi-rank is over there,' said Kathy. She looked up at him, the dreamy look still in her eyes and the throbbing music in her head. She sighed. 'I wanted it to go on for ever,' she said. She wrinkled her nose. 'Now, back to Elliot and duty.'

'Not just yet. I rang through during the interval and he was sleeping quietly. Becky was reading and about to go to bed, and said there was no need for us to hurry back.' There was a kind of lazy question in the dark eyes, and a smile on the mobile mouth that Kathy began to distrust. 'And I have to make sure you get back safely.'

Kathy glanced at him sharply. The evening had been relaxed and enjoyable, and maybe he was getting a false impression of her. Her laughter at some of the things that Johannes had said might have given the impression that she now approved of his company off duty, and was relaxed enough to get closer to either of them.

Sitting close to Michiel in the packed auditorium had meant physical contact that had both alarmed her and filled her with a strange and sensual warmth that had grown as the evening wore on. Johannes, on her other side, had kissed her cheek a couple of times and sat even closer than Michiel, but he gave her none of the sensation she received from the often silent man on her left side, and once, when Michiel had taken her hand for a minute or two, linking up with the others in the row of seats and swaying to the music, she had been disappointed when he had let her hand fall and gone back to studying the programme.

'I thought you were in a hurry to get away,' she said. 'We may have missed the best part of the concert.'

'We do have to check on Elliot, but I've had enough jazz and enough of Johannes for one evening,' Michiel said calmly. 'He has a habit of taking a lot for granted, and I wanted you to myself for a while. I'd hate to think that you took him too seriously.'

'What do you mean? I don't need protecting from Johannes. He's a great guy.' The dream faded and she missed the warm affection of Johannes' bear-hug in this uneasy tension now forming between her and Michiel. There was an edge of danger in her own charged emotions, and her mouth was dry.

'Sure, he's a great guy, but do you think it wise to give a comparative stranger a key to your apartment?' He didn't wait for a reply, but stepped into the road and whistled for a taxi that was cruising for passengers. He opened the door for her.

'There's no need for you——' she began, but he climbed in after her and slammed the door, telling the driver the name of the hotel on the Amstel. Kathy was annoyed. He spoke of Johannes as if he was a man of few morals, and yet she knew that Michiel was full of admiration for him as a personal friend and a very good doctor! Kathy glanced at him and resented the way he now seemed to think that she would do exactly as he suggesed, almost as if she was back in the clinic and working with him, but all the time her heart told her that it was true, this was what she wanted—to be with Michiel, to be needed by him, even if he broke her heart.

Knowing that she could never feel anything of love or sexual attraction for Johannes made their contact easy, as she could talk to him, laugh with him, and had enjoyed his swift brotherly hugs when he had been uplifted by the musical beat during the concert.

She glanced at the firm chin of the man beside her, and wondered if her relaxed and happy attitude at the jazz concert might have given the impression that she was falling in love with Johannes. A hint of a triumphant smile touched her lips. He looked like thunder, as if he might even be a tiny bit jealous.

The lights of night-time Amsterdam outlined bridges and lit the towers of ancient buildings. The sullen water of the canals was dark under the leafy banks, houseboats showed pale lamps or lay in darkness, and there was magic in the warm air. It was impossible to be cross, and Amsterdam at night was everything that she had been told.

She exclaimed in delight when she saw the Montelbaan Tower, floodlit. Michiel leaned forward and spoke to the driver, then sat back by her side. 'I never did show you the city,' he said. 'Night blurs the hard edges and makes everything beautiful, and the Dutch have a talent for showing off their treasures. They make everything sparkle like the diamonds that are so famous here.'

'I wonder if I'll have time to visit a diamond factory,' Kathy said.

'Do Elliot a favour and keep Becky occupied the day after tomorrow. He wants me take him to buy diamonds, and doesn't want her to know about it.' He grinned. 'Poor Elliot. He knows when he's beaten, and he wants to buy a ring here as it will be a good bargain and of the finest quality, but he can't quite make the decision yet. The ring may burn a hole in his pocket for months before he eventually gives it to her and asks her to name the day.'

'They'll be very happy, and Becky will feel secure,' said Kathy.

'Women do,' he said shortly. 'Why does a ring mean so much?'

'Where are we going?' Kathy ignored his remark and looked out of the window. She knew little about the city, but she could see that the taxi had changed course.

'I told him to drive by the Zeedijk and the old city wall. There are ships there, and the old tower called the Schreierstoren dates from the fifteenth century. It was built as part of the fortifications, but some say the name comes from the Dutch ''to cry out''. It stood astride the canal on the old city harbour, and was the place of embarkation of many sailors.'

'Why that name?'

'It has a legend that women gathered to say goodbye and to weep when their men sailed away. It was a tower of tears, and from the top they could see the ships go far away over the horizon.' He saw her solemn expression and squeezed her hand gently. 'Cheer up. They came back, or most of them did, and think what must have been the scene then with all those joyous reunions. From the tower they could see the ships returning, so it couldn't have been all tears.'

'It's sad and beautiful,' Kathy murmured. 'But any leaving is sad. Oh, Michiel, I shall leave England for two or three whole years, and now I don't know if I can bear it!'

They left the cab and Michiel told the driver to wait while they walked by the sea wall. 'You came here. That was a kind of leaving,' he said.

'That was different. I had to come away to sort out my life, but I left in too much of a hurry. Now I've found I can look back and wonder if it was wise to leave Beattie's for good. I have managed to forget a lot of things, and to think straight about my life, but I can't go back now. It wouldn't be the same, and I'd be embarrassed.'

'Is it only the hospital you miss? What about your friends?'

How could she say that she had fallen in love and wanted to stay with him or to follow wherever he led her, for love and not for duty? There was a sob in her voice. 'I have good friends, but after getting over Tim, it's been like a coming back to life after being numbed.'

'Like a limb or a hand that has been badly hurt.' His dark eyes were full of understanding and some personal sadness. 'I know all about that, too. The coming back to life often hurts more than the first injury, doesn't it? We all make mistakes, and mine was to think that I could change someone from a dear but weak girl to someone able to give up drugs and face a good future.'

'Did you love her very much?' asked Kathy.

'I loved her, but I was never in love with her. We were both very young and I thought I could change the world! I hate waste, and she wasted her life when we were sailing with friends in the Aegean when she swam out and never came back.'

'An accident?'

'No, she left a note.' His face was bitter. 'I tried too hard, and she said she wasn't strong enough to do what I wanted her to do. She had been without a fix for eight days, and it was too much.'

Kathy put a hand on his arm. 'You can't blame yourself for trying to help her,' she said softly, 'any more than you could do anything to save your little sister.' He looked at her sharply. 'I heard that she died of meningitis,' she said. 'It must have been awful.'

A low and warning sound came from across the water, repeated as they stood close together by the sea wall. It came again and sounded even more menacing. 'Fog out at sea,' said Michiel, and put an arm round her shoulders as she shivered, although she wasn't cold. He kissed her eyelids, and touched her hair, in which the mist was leaving tiny droplets that shone against the lamplight. 'You have diamonds in your hair, Kathy,' he said.

Light mist now snuffed out the lights of distant ships

anchored off the shore, and the taxi-driver coughed. 'We must go,' said Kathy, and gazed up at the tower wondering if through the fog she would ever hear the sound of weeping. I shall leave this place and look back with regret, she thought. My tears will add to the sorrow of the tower of tears, even if I am no longer here. I have finally washed away any feeling I had for Tim, but what have I in its place? I shall take away an emptiness, a longing for something more than just a sexual encounter with a man who is dedicated to his work, and who, after seeing so much of the seamy side of sex, must be wary about real love and unwilling to have any permanent commitment.

The hotel was quiet, and the huge cat didn't bother to open an eye when they passed the chair in the foyer on which he slept. 'Evil monster,' whispered Michiel. 'At least we know where he is, and he can't get anywhere near to Elliot.' He tiptoed past the cat with a finger to his lips.

'Why are we whispering? asked Kathy, stifling a giggle.

'It's so quiet and unreal at night here. The whole foyer should be covered in cobwebs and old Rip van Winkle there should be asleep for a hundred years,' suggested Michiel. 'It seems a pity to wake him.' They exchanged glances, and Kathy felt again the deep magnetic charisma of the man whom she was only now beginning to know and understand. The night porter sat nodding by the desk, and shook his head when Michiel asked if there were any messages for him.

'So there's no need for you to see Elliot,' Kathy said. 'Goodnight. See you tomorrow.' Michiel followed her and was behind her on the first stair.

He smiled. 'I want that night-cap you promised me,' he said.

'I didn't!' There was panic in her voice. She distrusted his air of confidence and the way his dark eyes regarded her.

'Hush, you'll wake the cat,' he said. 'I brought you safely home after being a city guide, and now I have fog in my throat and need a drink.'

'The bar is closed and they won't make coffee at this hour,' she whispered, but found that they were half-way up the stairs.

'You have a brand new fridge in your room with everything a thirsty man could need,' he said firmly.

'I ought to see Elliot,' she said.

'I'll do that. You mix me a whisky and water, and I'll be with you in five minutes. Spring water,' he insisted.

Kathy looked about her. While in her own room in Elliot's suite she could have entertained him in the neutral sitting-room, but this was her bedroom and the only place where she could entertain anyone without disturbing Becky or Elliot, who were beyond the thick wall dividing her separate room from the rooms within the suite.

She put away the nightie that the maid had draped seductively over the bed as if a very slim version of Kathy, with a nine-inch waist and voluptuous hips, was inside it, and she tucked back the cover that the maid had opened invitingly, ready for her to slip between the sheets. It all had a terribly come-to-bed air about it, with the shaded pink lamp at the side and the huge picture of a Fragonard pastoral scene above the bed. She breathed more easily. It now looked more impersonal, and when she had mixed the drinks and placed the glasses on each side of the small table and arranged the two chairs to match by the window—well away from the bed—*and* switched on all the lights, she felt safe.

The door was slightly open and she heard Michiel

close the door of the suite. He walked the few steps to her room and shut the door behind him. 'Sleeping like a baby,' he said. 'No trace of a wheeze, and I think he will be fine once we have him desensitised, as he isn't allergic to many proteins.'

'Is it to your liking?' Kathy asked as he took the first sip from his glass.

'A little watery,' he replied, and she got up and took his glass to the fridge to top up with more spirit. 'Obviously, you are not a barmaid.'

'I seldom mix drinks for men late at night in my room,' she said. 'I'm tired, and I'd like you to go as soon as you have drunk this.'

As she turned she found him close behind her. She gasped. Carefully, he took the glass and put it on top of the small fridge. His arms engulfed her and she was absurdly reminded of the picture of Jupiter in the guise of a dark cloud embracing a goddess, almost like the picture on the wall. His mouth came over her brow and cheeks in a teasing continuous kiss, and she leaned away as her trembling mouth was captured. She felt his hands caressing her throat, and then his lips on her shoulder through the thin cotton of her shirt, and she wanted to tear away the delicate material and guide his lips to her breast, but she knew that she must retain her sanity. This man was not for her! She glimpsed the filmy blue drapes at the window and clutched the memory of his face looking up at the girl in blue. If I give in now, I am lost forever, she thought with a sense of desperate loss. I would be just an easy conquest, to be enjoyed, discarded and forgotten.

'Kathy,' he murmured, and it was music and delight and the promise of desire that could be exquisitely fulfilled. She was aware of her tiny bikini pants and their discernible line under her skirt where his hands smoothed her taut hips, and the insistent mouth that teased and compelled her lips to open in submission. His kisses were more urgent, and he was drawing her into an ever closer embrace. A whirlwind of desire threatened to engulf her; desire that could only lead to insecurity and unhappiness. She broke away and her eyes were full of tears of anger.

'How could you? I have given you no cause to think you can do this to me!'

'You want me as much as I want you,' he said, and his voice was deep with passion. 'I've wanted to hold you in my arms for so long, Kathy. You allowed Johannes to kiss you, so why not me?'

'That is quite different,' she said. 'Johannes is just a friend, and I know it means nothing.'

Michiel smiled, and she backed away, scared of the triumph in his eyes. 'I'm glad,' he said softly. 'That means that this is not between friends? That this does mean something to you?' He saw her distress and his arms sank to his sides. 'Kathy, my darling girl, I would never hurt you. I don't know what stupid inhibitions you cling to, but there is no need. We want each other, and there is no reason why we shouldn't be happy together. Do you think it was easy to sit there and see Johannes pawing you all the evening and you seeming to enjoy it?' He pushed back his dark hair and his eyes blazed. 'He is my friend, but I wouldn't trust any woman alone with him.'

'It depends on the woman! If you judge women by the ones you have to treat, who take sex for granted with no thought of love, then I suppose you think that any girl is an easy lay! At least Johannes knows the dfference between girls who will and those who won't. He can guess that when he meets them for the first time. He told me so, and he knows that I would never sleep with him.'

He stepped back as if she had struck him. 'Do you seriously believe that I have sex with any woman I can get into bed, as Johannes does? Do you imagine that I keep a "little black book"? Surely you have more sense than that?' She shook her head, trying to deny it, but her lips couldn't form the words and he was too angry to listen.

He seized her by the shoulders, and she was shocked by the fury in his eyes. 'Look at me! I am a doctor, and I have a sense of responsibility. I have a great deal of affection for many women friends, even Helena, but I would never try to make love to any woman I didn't love.'

'But your work must make you cynical about love,' Kathy ventured. 'In a place like this, sex is taken for granted in a way that I could never do. We have hardly met, Michiel.' There was pleading in her voice, a cry for time to decide if his kisses were sincere.

'Haven't you ever liked a person whom you knew you must never touch in that way? Someone infectious? Even someone quite unworthy of your deeper emotions? Haven't you ever wished that they were not infectious? That you could be friends, even if there was a terrible barrier between you. Many of the people we meet *do* have sex appeal and considerable charm, but it doesn't mean we sleep with them or lose our feeling for genuine love.'

'I know that, but when I worked in Casualty I was afraid I would get used to other people's suffering and become hardened,' said Kathy. 'The same must apply to work among people who have lost their moral values.'

'Don't say that! Don't even think it! Many are infected

through no fault of their own. Think of the haemophiliacs infected with AIDS through what they thought were life-giving transfusions. Think of Marijke who is an innocent child. Our job is to help, and not to stand back and make comforting noises. It doesn't mean we would do as they do, but we give them objective care and compassion, which I suppose is a kind of love,' he said, and his eyes lost their anger.

He thrust his hands deep into the pockets of his jacket. 'You are a nurse, and yet you seem as obtuse as anyone who has never seen sickness or suffering. Didn't Beattie's teach you anything about compassion? I've come to love Marijke because she is so much like my own little sister.'

'Poor little mite,' said Kathy. 'She is such a lovely child. I could care for her quite easily. Is she very much like your sister?' Kathy felt ashamed of herself.

'I think that was one of the factors that made me decide to take up medicine, and when I saw Marijke, I knew that I must do what I could to save her from the life surrounding her.'

'What about her mother?' asked Kathy.

'Helena was frantic. She came to the clinic for her own check up, and when it was found she had a form of venereal disease—fortunately one that could easily be cured—she wondered if Marijke had used her towel and infected her eyes.' He sighed. 'Even in her way of life, they think that infections happen to other people and that they will never contract anything really bad. I know that many people believe that such infections can't be caught by sharing toilets and using the same towels, but I have seen some cases like Marijke when a towel has carried an infection that has been transmitted if used immediately after the infected person used it.'

'Nobody believes that they will be hurt until it

happens, and then, panic!' said Kathy.

Michiel nodded, and smiled. 'She brought the child along to Johannes, who consulted me when I came over one weekend. This infection and the guilt over Marijke convinced Helena that she must leave her profession and marry a man who has been a friend for years. I have been counselling her and trying to make her feel less guilty, and visiting her in her rooms. She is free from infection now, and leaves for Leiden soon, taking Marijke with her. Meanwhile, she has promised to take only carefully chosen clients who are fit.' He looked at Kathy with cold eyes. 'I shall miss her when I come back to Amsterdam. She can be very amusing, and at least she has a warm heart.'

He drank some more of his whisky and put the glass down firmly as if he was ending a meeting and was about to leave. 'I'm sorry if I offended you,' he said brusquely. 'I read the wrong signs, but when we stood together by the sea wall, I knew that we could be very happy together. Any man would want you, and once you can forget your inhibitions you will find that life has much to offer. You must not judge all men by one rejection and the blow to your pride.'

'I thought I was in love,' she said, but couldn't meet his gaze. It all seemed so long ago now, and so unimportant, and yet it was only a few months since she had finished with Tim.

'Love? You have an unawakened love that has been locked away and never given to any man, Kathy. It's in your eyes and the shape of your mouth, and when you kiss it hints at such wonderful depths of passion.' He spoke more quietly and with a hint of sadness. 'I know you better than you imagine.' He smiled wryly. 'You have shown quite clearly that you could never be satisfied with sex without love, but you have lost your faith and can't see the difference.'

'That's ridiculous. How could you know? We've known each other for such a short time.' Kathy stared at him with troubled eyes, sensing that he did know far more about her than she wished him to know.

'I saw you a long time ago and couldn't forget you.'

'At the rugby match?' She smiled in disbelief.

'I saw you again, remember, after that night of blood and guts and sheer strength of will, and I knew what kind of a woman you would become, and I saw your face when you kissed little Marijke.'

She shook her head and looked away. 'No,' she whispered. 'How could you know anything about the real me?'

'I saw the real you,' he said quietly, 'and love what I saw. But now, you confuse the issue by encouraging Johannes and never looking like a nurse! What's a man to think?' He looked annoyed as if he hated to find his judgement at fault. 'You aren't the type to go to Leiden with Johannes for a weekend. I know that, but this evening I began to think that he might persuade you. Believe me, Kathy, Johannes likes to make conquests, and if he swept you off your feet he'd hurt you badly.'

'You are a hypocrite, Michiel!' Kathy spoke in a clear but low voice. 'Isn't that exactly what you want? Isn't that exactly what you tried to do? Just that! You thought I was easy just because I let Johannes kiss me in a friendly manner and we laughed together. Sure, he's attractive and fun—and so is my cousin!'

'That was quite, quite different,' he said, in a low voice as if the admission pained him, and even surprised him. 'I do not have Johannes' track record, and I would never hurt you, Kathy.'

'Please go,' said Kathy faintly. 'I am sure that you have other people to visit and other things to do. At least Johannes took no for an answer, and I feel safe with him.'

'But you gave him a key!' He shook his head as if she were a slightly naïve child. 'If a woman gives a key to Johannes, he takes it for granted that she is willing to give much more.'

Kathy laughed. 'When he goes to London he'll meet Julia, and she just isn't his type. She is more likely to challenge him to arm-wrestling than to hop into bed with him! I did make it clear that I had a flatmate.'

'That should be a memorable meeting,' he said, and they both smiled, a trifle reluctantly. Kathy relaxed. The picture of Julia and Johannes in a clinch was too funny for words.

She laughed. 'So if you go to London, be warned. A bed on the settee or the floor and a rather grim lady who doesn't really care for men at all, unless they are fond of bird-watching on draughty estuaries, or climbing damp hills!'

He picked up his jacket.

'Goodnight,' Kathy said.

'Goodnight.' He held her lightly and kissed her lips softly. 'It isn't only Rip van Winkle downstairs who is asleep,' he whispered. 'What golden spell will bring you to life, Kathy?' He made no further attempt to touch her, and she followed him to the door to make sure that the safety-catch was fixed, and then turned to the empty room. The cushion on the chair on which he had been sitting when she had gone to freshen his drink was crushed against the back of the chair, as if he had just left it, and his whisky glass was not quite empty. Instinctively, she went to shake the cushion, then stopped.

She also left the glasses to be washed up in the morning, and when she awoke she smoothed the crushed cushion and ran her fingers over the empty glass as if he had only just left the room instead of all those hours before. It kept him there in her imagination just a little while longer. Kathy dressed and returned the room to its normal impersonal tidiness, and she felt as if she had lost something that could never be replaced. He will never try to make love to me again, she thought, and wished that she had lost her mind and heart and body under the soft rosy light and the sensuous painting above the bed.

Her hand was on the door when the telephone rang, and she sank down on the now tidy chair. 'When did this happen?' she asked anxiously.

'Soon after we came back to the hotel,' said Michiel. 'I left you and walked as I wanted to think and to have some fresh air. I got back to Johannes' place an hour later, and heard that he had been taken to hospital.'

'But what happened?' she asked.

'That terrible heap that he drives about Amsterdam because he refuses to put his good car at risk has very bad brakes. When he tried to move away from the concert among the dozens of cycles that students were riding away to their homes, he drove on to a bank and the car just tipped over into the water. I saw him in the ward and he has a fractured arm and bruising, but no lasting damage, but I think he will surely have to face charges for an unroadworthy vehicle. It wasn't exactly in showroom condition before the accident, and now it will go to the crusher.'

'I'll tell Elliot and try to get along to see him,' said Kathy. 'Poor Johannes.'

'I thought you'd want to know,' said Michiel briskly. 'Tell Elliot I'll see him after breakfast.'

The line went dead, and once again Kathy felt a sensation of loss. Michiel had done the polite thing, making sure that she knew so that she could tell Elliot, and from his tone she felt that they were back to a nursing sister and doctor relationship, helping a patient and showing interest in others by the way. Did he believe that she would rush frantically to the bedside of the injured man?

Elliot was shocked. 'I could have been given a lift in that death-trap,' he said. 'Just think, we could have killed if we had been with him!' Kathy stifled a smile. 'You must go and take some grapes or something,' he said vaguely. 'I feel quite well again, and Becky shall come with me to the Old Church and to do some shopping while you see how badly hurt that young man is.'

'Michiel will be here soon, and he can tell us more,' said Kathy, and Becky poured a fresh cup of coffee for Michiel as soon as they heard the lift doors.

'You shall take Kathy to see him so that she can report back to me,' said Elliot as soon as Michiel was buttering a croissant as if he had not eaten for many hours.

'More coffee?' asked Becky. 'I can never understand how a man in his position can drive such a car,' she said primly. 'I think it is very important that a man keeps up a certain standard.' Michiel smiled, and Kathy sensed that he felt, as she did, that Becky would make sure that she travelled first class in luxury cars for the rest of her life if she was given the chance.

'There's no need to rob you of your nurse,' said Michiel. 'If you need Kathy, I can bring you the latest news.'

'I would like to visit him,' Kathy said firmly. 'Johannes is a friend who made me feel at home here, and I shall take him some fruit and sweets.'

'In that case, you'd better be ready in fifteen

minutes,' said Michiel shortly. 'I haven't all day to waste, as I shall take over at the clinic today. This may change my plans, even if Hans will be back shortly, and he can take over as he would when Johannes is due to go to England.'

'I don't need you this morning, Kathy,' said Elliot. 'Feel free to stay as long as you like, and just ring through at lunchtime if you aren't back here by then. I hope we can still do that bit of business tomorrow, Michiel. The girls can go shopping and leave us in peace. You can take me to lunch in that nice club you mentioned, and we can ignore the ladies for once.'

'Well, I can use a good pair of hands today, if you can spare her,' said Michiel. 'Wear something that won't be ruined,' he said to Kathy. He glanced at her to assess her reactions. 'That is, if you don't feel obliged to dress up to visit Johannes, and want to spend the whole morning holding his hand.'

'I'll be ready,' Kathy said simply, although she was inwardly seething. Once more, he was taking it for granted that she would come when he called, and leave her leisured position for which she was being paid to join him in some unmentionable place doing something equally distasteful, but she had no intention of him having any cause to accuse her of refusing to help the needy. After all, wasn't that what fate had in store for her once she joined the VSO?

She hurried back to her room and locked the door. Jeans and sloppy sweater were all she could think of wearing after seeing the clinic, and she deliberately chose a top that was sludgy in colour and had seen better days. Her hair glowed, but her face was pale, and she hoped that she looked as unattractive as possible. Elliot turned up his nose at her trainers, and Michiel grinned as if he knew why she had dressed in such a way. Kathy hoped that he would not comment.

'A starched cap and apron would go nicely with that expression,' he said. 'I can see that the Third World will soon have a very serious worker who looks as if she has completely lost her sense of humour. Some girls would be pleased to be thought attractive, but I can feel the prickles from here!'

'You asked me to be ready,' she said sweetly. 'If I am to visit the sick and then work, I must make sure I wear nothing to distract the patients.'

'I've ordered a car,' he said. 'Come on.'

'The same hospital? I can see Marijke again?' Kathy suggested to break the silence.

'No, they took Johannes to a small private place in which we have shares. It's very good and we do some fine work—or the people we leave to run it do for us. I see it very seldom, but Johannes keeps an eye on it and the staff, and now he is glad to have a peaceful room to himself.' He glanced at her. 'He's a lot more shocked than I told Elliot, and he looks a bit of a mess.'

They stopped off to buy flowers from the beautiful flower market, and Kathy buried her face in masses of half-open roses. 'Heavenly,' she breathed. 'Quite my favourite flowers. It's a pity that Elliot is allergic to flowers, as Amsterdam has the best selection I've ever seen. I know we're too late for the bulb fields, but I think I prefer flowers like this instead of regimented rows on rows of the same colours.'

'An English rose,' Michiel said softly. 'Deeply red and sweet and slow to open, but wonderful when persuaded to yield its fragrance.'

'These are white and pink,' she pointed out, and blushed in spite of her efforts to ignore his words. She tried to laugh. 'This variety is safer. No thorns, and easy to set in place in a vase.'

The hospital was inside an old house behind the Herengracht. On the stepped roof were figures that showed that the house had once belonged to a merchant, and showed the coat of arms from the guild to which he belonged. Because it was the end house in a row, the windows let in more light than in the narrow houses at its side, and the airy room in which Johannes lay in bed looked over the canal and the distant sea.

Impulsively, Kathy hurried to the side of the bed and took the limp hand that lay on the pale pink coverlet. She was appalled. Gravel and dirt had scoured his face and he had deep cuts over both eyes. The cuts were now stitched and sealed with waterproof sealant, and the bruises were yet to take on many colours, but Johannes was almost unrecognisable.

He tried to smile, but his bruised lips could not move freely and he spoke softly in Dutch as if the effort to think in English exhausted him.

Kathy felt at a loss. She spoke very little Dutch, and he seemed to have withdrawn from being the bilingual and vital man she knew to this weak and very Dutch patient. She held his hand and he gave an answering squeeze. Kathy bent to kiss the one patch of his face that wasn't bruised, and he nodded slightly. 'I'll come back again,' she promised, sensing that he was sedated and needed sleep above all other needs. He closed his eyes and Michiel led her away, leaving the roses to the care of the nurse in charge.

Michiel turned to her in the shaft of sunlight that met them at the door. 'Tears for Johannes,' he said quietly. 'What a lucky man.' He wiped the tears from her cheeks with a clean white handkerchief that smelled of tweed and old bus tickets.

'He looks terrible,' she gulped. 'It's twice the shock when it's someone I know.'

'He's fine. The fracture is a simple one, and he'll be able to travel as he planned, but you'll have to warn your friend—no arm wrestling,' he added, and Kathy smiled a watery smile. 'He is concussed, and they are going to X-ray his skull, but I think he's avoided a bad head injury, and he'll be better in a day or so.'

'Now what do you want me to do?' Kathy hated the thought of having time on her hands.

'Can you bear the clinic again?' he asked, with more hesitation, as if he now considered her opinion.

'If there's work to be done, we must make sure that nobody suffers because Johannes is out of action,' she said.

'Good girl.' He walked away from the house. 'It isn't far, and we can pick up some things on the way that are needed from the pharmacy.'

Kathy followed, strangely content to be with him, knowing that they would agree about professional matters and enjoy working together whatever emotions lay under the surface. She saw the gleam in his eyes that told her that he was happy in her company, and his light touch on her arm stirred deep longing, but no tension.

It isn't much, but it will have to do, she considered. Just for a week or so before he goes out of my life for ever. She bit her lip. A love that never was might be forgotten in time.

'Cheer up,' said Michiel. 'Whatever it is may never happen, or so someone once told me.'

'I know,' said Kathy. 'I do know.' She tried to smile. 'I hold the next patient if he's under eleven stone,' she said. 'No more minor surgery for me.'

'I'm getting you trained for medicine in a mud hut,' he replied. 'That would really be worth seeing.'

'Drop in if you're passing,' she said lightly, and

wished with all her heart that they could go together. Her dreams of adventure had faded, and she couldn't believe that she had agreed to leave all that was familiar and dear to her.

'Who knows? You might change your mind and go back to London,' he suggested, and kissed the tip of her nose.

CHAPTER EIGHT

'CAN you tell her about the baby clinic at the hospital?'
Kathy looked hot and upset. 'I'm so frustrated at not
being able to speak to her about her baby and that rather
nasty rash on the poor little bottom.'

Michiel looked up from the note he was writing and
grinned. 'I thought you knew some Dutch,' he said
heartlessly.

'A few words, but what is the Dutch for zinc and
castor oil ointment? That's the cheapest and best thing I
could think of for someone who can't afford much.'

'Search me. I don't know either until I look it up.' He
reached for a pharmacopoeia. 'You're right. For a long
time, good old Z and C was discarded in favour of new
and much more expensive preparations, but it's coming
back in favour and all the best people now wear white
zinc as a sun-block on the ski-slopes. *They* think it's
new.'

He scribbled a prescription and handed it to her. He
then scribbled another note, and she saw that it was the
address and times of the clinics at the hospital. 'Thank
you,' Kathy said, and hurried back to the woman with
the grizzling baby. The woman smiled and Kathy gave
the baby a pat on the cheek and a bright, empty, rigid
plastic container to take away as a toy.

The sun was hot through the glass and all her efforts to
open the window had failed, so Kathy wedged the door
open and cleared away the tray she had used for a
dressing earlier. She brushed back her untidy hair and

wished that she could take a cool shower, but there was more work to do. Steam from the discoloured fish-kettle now clouded the window in the clinical room, and she turned down the gas jet. A row of clean instruments lay ready to put away, and she dried the last batch to add to them.

'Feel at home? Just like the casualty department at Beattie's?'

Kathy gave Michiel a dirty look. 'With this equipment? You have to be joking. I don't know how I came to be bullied into coming here.'

'C'mon! Where's that pioneer spirit that is taking you into the jungle?' He grinned. 'I'm being very good to you, giving you a taste of the joys to come and teaching you that all those glittering machines that once seemed essential are not necessary.'

'I'm learning,' she admitted ruefully. 'It's incredible what I can do with two pairs of forceps and a small roll of sterile gauze.'

'I hope you didn't waste any.' She glanced up sharply, ready to retort, but saw that he was laughing and she blushed under the warmth of his smile. 'You have done wonders,' he said. 'Turn off the gas and wash your hands, and we'll get some coffee.'

'Here?' Kathy wrinkled her nose.

'No. I never eat or drink here unless I have to. There's a Brown Café along the road, and we can sit on the canal-bank and perhaps have a sandwich, as I'm hungry and yet haven't time for lunch.'

'A Brown Café? They certainly are brown, but look so dark and dingy.'

Michiel laughed. 'They are traditional, and some say the brown colour on the panelling is only partly varnish and that eighty per cent is tobacco smoke from the terrible shag that the sailors used over the years.'

Kathy combed her hair and then pulled it back through the rubber band that had held it rather unsuccessfully away from her face all the morning. Tendrils of curling brightness escaped, and when Michiel saw her he smiled gently. He reached across and pulled the band away with a snap. 'Give it back!' Kathy demanded. 'It keeps my hair tidy.'

'Correction. It did its best, but haven't you heard? Tight ties can make you go bald!' He smoothed down the soft hair and his touch was an aching balm. 'Besides, you don't want to be busted again, do you? Carrying what could be a tourniquet and smelling of surgical spirit?'

'Oh, do I smell of that? The stopper came out with a rush and I had it all down my jeans.'

'I won't offer you perfume this time, or our rather pleasant morning might be ruined,' he replied, and took his hand away from her hair, as if it wanted to remain but he knew it was not allowed to do so.

Kathy looked away. All morning they had worked hard and with perfect harmony, seeming to know exactly what the other wanted and wasting no time. All the patients had been seen, notes had been written, and Kathy had been able to make sure that the woman employed to clean the floors had done the job well. It seemed that they had got through so much work, and it was still only just after two o'clock, too late for coffee and even an early lunch.

'What does *Vrouw* mean?' she asked when at last they sat under a shady tree and watched the barges float by the canal-bank and disappear under the bridge. 'Some of them called me *Mevrouw*, which I know is Mrs, and some the Dutch for Miss, but the last man said something *"uw vrouw, uw mooi vrouw."* He said it several times to you, but I'm sure he was talking about me.'

Michiel sipped the strong black coffee and watched

her face. 'You really didn't understand? I would have thought that his tone might have told you.' He laughed, then added brown sugar to his coffee and reached for the cream. 'I think I need cream today. Would you like to walk along the canal after this?'

'That would be nice,' she said, but persisted. 'I wasn't watching his face. I was bandaging his arm, remember. I guessed at a lot that was said, but when some words are similar it is difficult to know what they mean. Some languages are very odd, and even an inflection of the voice can mean something quite wrong and might give offence. What did he mean?'

'Nobody said anything to give offence to you, Kathy,' he replied. 'It means beautiful wife.' She blushed deeply and he looked teasing. 'They were all very appreciative.' He grinned. 'Even the old meths drinker who had lice.'

'Don't.' Kathy shuddered. 'I hope he uses that stuff you gave him, but I doubt it, unless he thinks he can drink it! Poor old thing. Does he really sleep rough for seven months of the year?'

'They do in London and Paris and New York, and everywhere in the world where they can find no permanent home. Some like it and hate being put into hostels, so I didn't suggest it. He has a right to live as he pleases, as long as it doesn't hurt anyone but himself.'

'But what if he has a family somewhere? They must wonder where he is and how he is faring.'

'Are families important? ' His brown eyes were serious.

'Oh, yes!' Urgency and conviction were in Kathy's steady gaze. 'I lost most of mine, but I know they loved me, and even when my father was so ill, just being together was important. When I have my own family I shall——' She stopped, aware of the question in his eyes.

'That will be after you've healed all the sick and

starving in Africa or India, or wherever they send you? Don't leave it too long, Kathy. One day, you might look up and find it's too late.' He touched her hand and she wanted him to draw her into his arms and hold her safe against the future.

'I have plenty of time,' she said, but her heart beat faster. Why don't I know you, really know what goes on behind those heavenly dark eyes? she thought passionately, and she knew that she would give up all her plans if Michiel could be sincerely in love with her and not just after a light affair that would lead to nothing but her heartbreak.

He poured more coffee. 'Plenty of time,' he echoed. 'But why waste it?'

'You do good here, and back in London. What's the difference? I hope I, too, shall do good wherever I am needed.' The lift of her chin showed her determination. 'I ought to ring through and see if Elliot wants me later,' she said, and left her coffee while she found a telephone and made the call.

'Any crisis?' Michiel asked when she returned. she was aware of him watching her as she walked slowly back to the table, and she felt as if her legs were heavy and clumsy as she tried to appear unselfconscious. Two girls sitting on the next bench were cool and fresh and pretty in cotton dresses, and she was aware that she smelled of meths, her shirt was crumpled and her jeans needed a wash.

'Nothing,' Kathy said. 'I ought to go back, but he seemed to want to be left to rest and asked if we can go with him to an Indonesian restaurant tonight.'

'Has he booked a table? The best ones get very busy.'

'He said he had booked one by the flower market. What's so special about Indonesian food?' Kathy wanted to know.

'I advise you to treat this sandwich as your last meal before tonight.' He got to his feet. 'You can have more coffee,' he offered generously, 'but dinner will be a marathon meal and I shall have to loosen my belt if I stay the course, or rather, the very many courses on offer. Everything they serve is delicious and tempting. You'll enjoy it.' He looked at her with an enigmatic expression that made her blush. 'I shall enjoy it, too.' He glanced at the two girls who were laughing, their dresses stirring in the breeze, showing long brown legs and sandalled feet. 'Wear something pretty,' he commanded, and smiled at the girls.

Kathy bit her lip and felt even more grubby and dishevelled. It was no use trying to convince herself that it was not her fault that she was looking at her worst. She was like this just because Michiel had made her work in the clinic. It wasn't fair! Tonight he would expect her to look pretty and to smell a little better than she did now! He wanted both sides of the coin, made to his satisfaction. Now, she told herself, through no fault of my own, I feel inferior to those two smartly dressed idle creatures who seem to think they know him, and he is contrasting me with them.

Michiel put up a hand in recognition of the two girls, and they walked over, addressing him in Dutch and eyeing Kathy with ill-concealed curiosity. He made brief introductions and they went away, walking towards the main street. 'Friends?' asked Kathy, suddenly suspicious that they might be girls from the red-light district. If he was on friendly terms with one of the women there, then why not others?

'Night-nurses,' he replied. 'They said they had such a bad night at the private hospital that they decided to make the most of the sunshine and sleep later. They also said that Johannes has been very sick and they are taking more X-rays of his skull.'

He gathered up the coffee-tray and took it back to the café, and when he returned he stood by the bench as if waiting for her to leave also. 'Go shopping or back to the hotel,' he suggested. 'I'll meet you all there later, and we can leave for the restaurant together.'

'There's a bit more clearing up to do,' Kathy began.

'No need,' said Michiel. 'It's better than it's looked for months, and I shall make sure everything is ready for use.'

'If Elliot doesn't need me, I can come back with you,' she said.

'No. You take the time off. I have to see someone.'

Kathy picked up her bag. 'Fine,' she said through stiff lips. 'I'll call in and see Johannes, and then go back to the hotel. Becky might want to go out, and I can read a good book while she is shopping.' She walked away with dignity. All the time he had been working with her he must have known he had other plans. Was this the day when Helena was due to leave for the country? Have I hurried and worked hard, not recognising his undercurrent of urgency? she thought. She glanced at her watch. They had got through the work in record time. She saw that his hair was damp, as if he had combed it with a wet comb to tame the thick locks. As she boarded the tram, she remembered that he had come from the men's room wearing the over-bright tie once more, and that both nurses had looked at him flirtatiously, as if they both really fancied him.

Kathy brushed back her hair and tried to put him out of her thoughts. If Helena was leaving, then he was sure to want to help her, but his care seemed very much more than a simple doctor-patient feeling. It was unusual for any medic to take time off to ferry his patient to the station with such solicitous care.

Johannes was lying flat, and a portable X-ray machine was being trundled away as Kathy tapped on the door of his room. His skin had a greyish tinge and his breathing was shallow. 'Johannes?' she said softly, and the nurse hovering behind her put a finger to her lips when Kathy turned to her with an enquiring glance. They left the room and spoke softly, and from the fractured English that the nurse could produce Kathy gathered that Johannes had tried to get out of bed in the night and fallen again, as if he lacked co-ordination.

The white plaster encasing his right arm was neatly applied and his fingertips were warm and pink, showing that the circulation of blood was not restricted, but his face was badly scratched and the bruising over one cheek was now a dull blue and yellow mass. That, together with the greyish colour, made Kathy long to be put in the picture as to his condition, and she wished that she could understand all that was said to her. It was impossible not to compare his appearance with accident cases she had met at Beattie's. It was impossible not to think that he might have a fractured skull, and that the shallow respirations and the inert form might be the signs of pressure of the fractured bone on a vital part of the brain.

The man walking quickly towards them stopped and said something to the nurse before going into the room. Kathy faced the closed door and knew that she had no right to enter. To them she was just a visitor, even if they knew that she was a nurse and a friend of Michiel's. A wave of emotion threatened to make her cry. Dear Johannes, her only real friend in Amsterdam, who had seemed to be bubbling over with life, rugged good looks and male virility when she had seen him return to the concert. Was it only yesterday? She had no idea how long she waited there, half hoping that she would be asked why she was there. A covered dressing-trolley went into the room, and another doctor joined the first one.

Two porters pushed a trolley along the corridor, and she stood aside to let them pass, but they stopped outside the door, and a minute later she saw Johannes, now unconscious, with an intravenous drip in his good arm. An intertracheal tube protruded from his bruised lips to make an efficient airway that could be connected to any anaesthetic he might have to be given, and he was being wheeled carefully to the elevator.

'Decompression?' she asked clearly as the nurse returned to make the bed.

'Ja.' Kathy helped her to strip off the bedclothes and to remake the bed with fresh linen, ready to receive the patient from the theatre, although it was more likely that Johannes would have to go to the recovery ward or intensive care after the surgeon had removed the splinter of bone that the nurse now showed Kathy on the X-ray picture.

'I will leave the telephone number of the hotel where I am staying,' said Kathy slowly, and the girl nodded and took the note and put it in her pocket.

'You are the woman friend or the *vrouw*?' asked the nurse. Kathy looked puzzled. 'The wife?' the girl said, as if unsure of the word.

'A friend,' said Kathy. 'Just a friend.' The nurse nodded and smiled in a knowing way. 'He has many friends,' she said. Kathy stared out of the window at the glinting water of the canal. Just a friend, she thought. Has Johannes any close female friends? He had girls whom he took and discarded, girls with whom he worked, but none close enough to stay with him and hold his hand or to weep for him. 'I'll come back later and wait,' Kathy said firmly. She walked quickly away and blinked in the bright sunlight of a music-filled city that seemed oblivious to the fact that a man lay unconscious with little pulse, and maybe even no will to fight for life.

Angrily she shook away the idea. Johannes would be fine, and he had everything to live for. He had a future that many men would envy, and he could have as many women as he could beckon to come into his web if he recovered. She stifled her tears as she sat staring out of the window of the tram. What if Johannes emerged saved, but with the mind of a vegetable? She left the tram and hurried back to the hotel, to find Elliot and Becky sitting very close together on the settee. They looked at her as if she was intruding, and she burst into tears.

Becky eyed the grubby jeans and sweater and turned up her nose at the lingering odour of spirit, but came to Kathy and put an arm round her shoulders. Between sobs, Kathy told them about Johannes, and Elliot asked if Michiel had been told.

'No. I left him after the clinic and he had a date,' Kathy said, recovering her voice. 'He knows that Johannes was having more X-rays, but not that he was taken to the theatre. I said I'd go back to the hospital later. Is that all right, Elliot?'

'Of course.' He looked at her with real concern. 'I had no idea you were so devoted to the man,' he said.

'Have a cool shower and change, and you'll feel better,' suggested Becky.

'I'll ring round and try to find Michiel,' said Elliot. 'Do as Becky told you, my dear.' He picked up the phone. 'Have you any idea where he might be? Not at the private hospital, as you came from there. Maybe at the general hospital, or even at the flat he shares with Johannes.'

'I have no idea,' said Kathy. She tried to smile. I can't say that he is helping a prostitute to get away to the country, she thought. It would sound too odd for words! And yet I'm sure that that's what he is doing. 'I'll get out of these things and freshen up,' she said.

From her room she heard Becky talking on the telephone, and knew that she was trying to locate Michiel. The tears that Kathy shed had done more to make Becky her friend than anything else she might have done. Kathy managed a weak smile as she turned on the shower and let the cool water flow over her shoulders and between her breasts. She also felt slightly embarrassed. So Elliot and Becky thought she was in love with Johannes, and the man at the clinic had pictured her as Michiel's wife. At least Becky knows that I am no threat to her, Kathy thought as the sweet-scented shampoo bubbled into a sensuous rivulet from her head to her feet. She gasped as the hot water stung her back, and then winced as the cold dash to invigorate her body made her reach for her towel.

'That's better.' Becky eyed her with approval. 'I've brought some tea, and we can have some in your room. Elliot is having a nap and wants to save his energy for this evening.'

'This evening?' Kathy stared.

'We are dining at an Indonesian restaurant, remember?'

'But I can't go out and enjoy myself until I know if Johannes is safely over the operation.'

'Elliot insists that you come. He's still a little nervous of hot rooms with flowers, but I've arranged a table by the window away from the flower market, and after the shower last night there won't be any free pollen about.' Becky poured tea and handed Kathy a plate of biscuits. 'In any case, what can you do for Johannes? You can leave the telephone number of the restaurant with the hospital, and they can send you news.' Becky looked at her slyly. 'Naturally, they'll want to know if you are a relative or a dear friend. If they are anything like our local hospital, they'll refuse to give any information to mere acquaintances.'

'Michiel will want to know,' said Kathy. 'He can find out what is happening. Did you contact him, Becky?'

'No.' Becky looked worried. 'I hope he hasn't forgotten tonight. They said he had gone to the station. You don't think he might have gone to Leiden or somewhere and forgotten, do you?'

'It's more likely that he's gone to see someone off on the train,' said Kathy.

'You aren't wearing that?' Becky looked at the plain brown skirt and sweater that Kathy flung on the bed. 'This evening we have to dress up and look our best. Elliot likes pretty things.' Becky opened the wardrobe wide and pulled out a pretty voile dress with a subtle flower print on the softly draped skirt. She dived below the dresses and found high-heeled sandals of rose-pink and green that picked out the colours in the dress. 'Now, this is pretty,' she said with an air of satisfaction. Kathy laughed. It was plain that Becky now wanted the girl she had considered a rival to look good.

'I can't wear that to the hospital,' said Kathy.

'You can, and then be ready to follow us to the restaurant. Just think if Johannes woke up and saw you looking beautiful.' Becky sighed. 'It would be so romantic.'

Kathy refrained from comment. Why ruin this new relationship with the jealous woman by denying that she and Johannes were lovers? Meekly, she dressed in the flowing voile and pinned a gold and sapphire brooch to her low neckline, and when she gave a mischievous twirl and arched her foot to show off the sandals Becky was delighted.

The porter rang the suite to say a message had come from the hospital to let them know that Johannes was out of Theatre and was "as well as could be expected". Kathy shrugged. That phrase could mean everything or nothing. How often she had been instructed to give just that amount of information to people enquiring after patients.

'I must go and find out more,' she said.

'I'll ring for a taxi, but promise to be at the restaurant tonight. You *are* still working for Elliot, and he would never forgive you if you missed this evening.'

Kathy nodded and filled a large handbag with essentials of make-up and tissues and money that she might need over the next few hours. She added a paperback, a light scarf and a jacket of pale green wool and went down to the waiting taxi.

In the foyer, she asked the receptionist if there had been any messages for or from Dr Michiel Raynor, but there was nothing. Kathy shrugged. There was no reason for Michiel to bother with her when an enchanting child had his full attention.

Kathy fumbled in her purse for the taxi fare, and a minute later was at the desk in the foyer of the private hospital. A man in a white coat walked past slowly and eyed her with interest. He smiled, and she was reminded of Johannes and his appraising glances at any girl pretty enough to merit a second glance. Suddenly, she felt overdressed and conspicuous. The breeze from the open door stirred the many handkerchief points of her skirt and then pressed them to her brown legs. 'Dr Johannes Wittener?' she asked.

A hand that was firm and almost painful in its grip turned her to face Michiel. 'Visiting the sick?' he asked in a hard voice. 'You really made an effort for him. What, no grapes or flowers? But dressed like that he'll never notice the lack of goodies.'

Kathy pulled away from him. 'I changed for this evening,' she said in a cold voice. 'I doubt if Johannes will be able to see me if he's still under sedation. You do know about the surgery?'

'Surgery?' Michiel dropped his hands to his sides and stared. 'No, I've only just now returned.'

'From the station? How are Helena and Marijke? Safely tucked into a train?' Kathy managed a smile.

'To hell with that! How is Johannes?' He left her and spoke rapidly in Dutch to the girl, who nodded and picked up a house phone. Kathy saw that Michiel now wore a rather elegant pale grey necktie of silk with a muted pattern of small dots of darker grey. The girl looked up and smiled.

'What did she say?' asked Kathy.

'We can go up. Come on, don't just stand there.'

Kathy hurried as fast as she could, wearing the high heels, and wished that her skirt was made of heavier material. She remembered now why she rarely wore it, as it flew up when she hurried or when a breeze caught the skirt—so much so that a doctor at Beattie's had compared her to the picture of Marilyn Monroe standing over a hot-air vent. Michiel paused to see if she was with him and looked back. Desperately, Kathy pushed the skirt down and tried to appear composed, and he watched her with amused interest, but a tiny pulse beating under his right eye gave away the tension he felt.

'So you do have legs! I'd almost forgotten, and yet they were the first things I saw when I met you in Amsterdam. I think they look better today. A bit untidy, I thought, sprawled on a bedroom floor with your shoes kicked off in abandon.'

'I am never abandoned,' she said with as much dignity as she could muster.

'Regretfully, no,' he agreed.

A nurse rose from her seat at the desk in the corridor and escorted them along to the recovery room. 'Not intensive care?' Kathy breathed a sigh of relief and Michiel looked at her sharply.

'You do care about him,' he said.

'Of course. He's been a good friend to me in Amsterdam, and I'm very fond of him.'

The nurse tapped softly on the door of a side room, and it was opened by the special nurse who had a chart in her hand on which she had made notes of Johannes' progress since he had returned from the theatre. Kathy went to the bedside and looked down at the pale face on the pillow. Johannes had a better colour. Even though he was pale, the greyness had gone; the bruising stood out dramatically, but his respirations were deeper and more even. Kathy touched his good hand, as she would if she was nursing him, to see if he was warm enough or if the tissues were limp and needing fluid. The nurse smiled, seeing only a girl dressed beautifully, visiting a man she loved and wanting to touch him.

Michiel bent over the bed and gently lifted Johannes' eyelids. He stood back satisfied. 'Good. He should be fine,' he said. 'You'll soon have him with you in London.'

'It was a routine decompression?' asked Kathy. 'No permanent damage?'

'Just pressure removed, and he's fine. He'll be as good as new and as randy as ever.' Michiel watched her face and Kathy tried not to show any emotion. Johannes stirred and moved his head as if it hurt. Instinctively, Kathy bent over him as if she was the special nurse. Johannes opened one eye and focused on her face.

'Hello, angel,' he said. 'I've got one hell of a hangover.'

'Go to sleep,' Kathy said. 'I'll come tomorrow when you are rested.' She turned away, tears of gladness in her eyes. Dear, amiable Johannes, who gave her such a comfortable feeling of affection and friendship.

'We must go. We are only in the way now,' said Michiel. He glanced at his watch. 'Elliot is dining early, and they'll expect us in an hour. We'll go straight to the restaurant and if you're good I'll buy you a drink.'

'I can go back to the hotel and go with them,' Kathy said. 'You don't have to stay with me in your off-duty time.'

He grinned. 'You are all dressed up and so am I, so why waste it? Let's show Amsterdam just how smart we Brits can be when we aren't covered in goo and meths, and when we bother to wash behind the ears.' He glanced at her shoes. 'I have a car so we'll drive. Can't have you breaking one of those pretty ankles.' He took her hand. 'The car park is badly surfaced, and you usually wear trainers,' he insisted gravely, but his eyes were laughing.

He parked by the side of the flower market, and they strolled along watching the flower sellers pack up for the evening. In a small bar, they watched the passing throng of students, local people and tourists flow past as if on a frieze. Kathy had a sense of unreality. Michiel seemed relaxed, but under his calm she sensed a kind of anger. He ordered *jenever* and made her drink the tiny glassful of juniper-gin in one gulp.

'It's powerful,' she said.

'But typically Dutch and, as this is I think a farewell drink, I want you to remember it. Remember that we are a mixture of light and shade, Kathy, soft and harsh. At first sip, *jenever* seems innocent, but taken as it should be, boldly and without reservations, it is strong and warming and unforgettable, just as Dutch men can be.'

'You said a farewell drink—are you leaving?' She

pretended to choke over her drink so that she could hide her dismay.

He took a long envelope from his pocket and handed it to her. 'I called in at the hotel and they gave me this for you. I am not leaving yet, but I think you are. This is from VSO, if I'm not mistaken.' He raised his glass. 'To your future, in a little mud hut somewhere in the Third World.'

Kathy slid her finger under the opening and unfolded the papers with a shaking hand. 'No mud hut,' she said. 'I am being sent to the Sudan to a refuge for orphaned children.' She dared not meet his gaze, but wondered how long it took for a heart to break. 'I must get back to England and sort out my gear.'

'When do you leave?'

'In two weeks' time.'

'Have you had all your jabs? I can do them, if you like,' he offered.

'Thank you. That would save time.'

'I'll bring what is necessary for the Sudan to the hotel tomorrow, and you can have them before you leave.'

'Michiel . . .' she began, but knew that she could never say what was in her heart. 'Thank you,' she said lamely.

He laughed harshly. 'Eat your heart out, Johannes, She's leaving us just when we need her most.'

'You have more staff now. You can manage,' she said.

'We'll manage,' he agreed. 'But that's not everything. Look, there's Becky, looking very anxious.' He forced a more genuine smile. 'Her feet are giving her hell.'

CHAPTER NINE

'YOU don't seem overjoyed.' Becky looked at Kathy with interest tinged with a trace of her usual malice.

'Of course I want to go,' Kathy asserted, but her hands were cold and she could hardly remember the events of the evening. Music had played softly, the lights were warm and rose-hued, and she had been seated opposite the man she now knew was more to her than her profession, her other friends and her future. What she did recall with heartbreaking clarity was the way his hair fell in a swathe that refused to stay back and his eyes glinted darkly in the soft light. She remembered the way that his hands rested on the table, the short nails immaculate and the strong sinews of his wrists jutting from the snowy cuffs under the lightweight grey suit.

Silly to recall that, when she was aware of so much more that was hidden, and knew just how his arms would feel around her, how his body would tense at it had that evening in her bedroom when she had resisted him. Fool! she thought bitterly. What did it matter if he only wanted her for the moment? He *had* wanted her, and she . . . Kathy tried to smile.

'It's just that the news took me by surprise,' she said bravely.

'But you've known for ages that the call would come soon,' said Becky. 'Have some Perrier? I always get thirsty after drinking wine, and it looks as if Elliot will keep Michiel talking in there for a long time.' She looked at the closed door of the bedroom. 'They're up to no good. They are going out together tomorrow, and I am not invited.' She sniffed. 'Michiel is taking him to some exclusive club for lunch, and I'm dying to see what it's like there. Not only that, I know when Elliot is being devious, and he won't even tell me what he wants to buy. He knows I adore shopping.'

'Maybe it's a present for you,' suggested Kathy, and hoped that Becky would change the subject before she guessed that Elliot was going to visit a diamond factory.

'He said that we must amuse ourselves and have lunch somewhere nice,' Becky admitted. 'I shall spend a fortune on a meal just to spite him.'

'I have to pack my things,' Kathy began.

'Your plane doesn't go until Friday, the day after tomorrow, which gives you plenty of time to come out with me, visit Johannes a couple of times and then pack.' She laughed. 'I promise not to slip syringes into your luggage, and you will be travelling first class all the way. Elliot insisted.'

'Johannes will soon be better,' said Kathy. 'Once a piece of bone like that is removed and the pressure is relieved, patients can sit up and eat normally in a very short time.'

'Would he be well enough to travel with you?'

'Why should he do that?' Kathy looked puzzled and then remembered that Becky and Elliot both believed that she was in love with Johannes. 'It would worry him to leave his patients now,' she said hastily. 'He's coming to England soon and will be staying in my apartment.'

'But you are going away.' Becky looked at her with doleful blue eyes. 'How can you go away and leave the man you love? I know how I felt when Elliot was so ill, and I think I'd die if anything happened to him now.'

Kathy looked out of the window, over the gently lapping water across to the lights on ships and the string of diamond brightness outlining the bridge. She thought of the 'tower of tears' and the women who watched their men leave for distant and hazardous shores long ago. This time, she was the one leaving, but the anguish would be the same, as this parting would be forever.

She had loved and nursed her father, but his death had been expected and a part of the continuation of life, a grief that was full of fond memory. This emptiness was a throwing away of something as yet untasted.

'Yes,' she said softly. 'Leaving someone you love is a kind of dying.'

'Lucky man.'

She swung round and saw Michiel bend to pick up a magazine that had fallen to the floor. She couldn't see his face, and when he put the pile of books and papers straight again his mouth was set in a hard line and his eyes were inscrutable, as if he was firmly under control.

'Has Elliot settled for the night?' asked Becky. 'I'll just pop in and make sure he has everything he needs.'

'He's fine, but he wants to say goodnight to you,' said Michiel. 'We are going out together at about eleven tomorrow, and I'll make sure he doesn't get over-excited.'

Kathy edged towards her own room. She was scared of the sudden passion in his eyes. Becky closed the door to Elliot's room behind her, and Michiel came towards her. She looked up at him and saw the passion subdued into a smouldering and painful control as he set his jaw and took her by the shoulders.

'You're hurting me,' she whispered, but the hurt went deeper than the grip on her soft flesh.

'You are a fool, Sister Tyler,' he said. 'Are you really leaving? Are you running away again?'

'I'm not running anywhere,' she retorted. It was easier now that he was angry. 'I am going to a job for which I have waited for months.'

'But do you think you are falling in love with Johannes?' He gave a wry smile. 'He's not exactly the faithful sort, and the tears you shed for him will not make him any different.'

'Johannes must do as he pleases,' said Kathy. 'I have given up trying to tell you that I am not in love with him. It's quite simple. I have an agreement that I must honour. I made a promise to serve overseas if they want me, and I can't let them down now.'

'Yes. That, I understand,' said Michiel. 'I don't think you would break your word, or a contract, whether it be work or . . . marriage.'

Her eyelashes hid the pain in her eyes. 'I have to go,' she said in a whisper.

'Then remember this.' His mouth found her own in a shattering union of frustration and sadness, and she sank against his arms as if all life was sucked out of her. The glass chandelier was like a galaxy of enchanted stars above her head. 'Goodbye, Kathy. I hope you know what you are leaving behind; what could have been. I wish I'd never met you, or arranged for Elliot to choose you as his nurse,' he added in a whisper that she only half heard, as his lips were hidden in her hair. He released her and lifted her chin in his hands tenderly. 'I do know about promises. Come back when you can, if you can, but don't expect the world to stand still while you are away.'

'Michiel?' she whispered desperately, but there was no time for explanations. The door to Elliot's room opened and Becky came back. Michiel lifted a hand in farewell and closed the other door as he left the suite.

'Elliot is nearly asleep,' said Becky. 'Cheer up. It may be very nice out there with all those naked under-nourished babies.' She shrugged. 'Rather you than me, but you can cope, I'm sure. Go to bed. You look worn out. Breakfast here at nine, and as soon as Elliot and Michiel have left we'll take a taxi and window-shop before lunch.' Becky gave a sigh of exasperation. 'You aren't listening. Surely you can't be that tired?'

He arranged my coming here? Kathy tried to recall what Michiel had said, then saw that she was being watched with curiosity, so she determinedly cleared her mind. 'Where do we have lunch?' she asked.

Becky chuckled. 'Elliot suggested that we take a short trip out of Amsterdam for lunch, and I heard that there are lots of nice shops for souvenirs in Marken, which is on the Usselmeer and not too far from here.'

Kathy brightened. 'I'd like to go there. Isn't that the place they used to call the Zuyder Zee? The women wear local costumes even when they don't have tourists there, and I'd like to take a few more photographs before I leave here.'

'You'll have to take your films home to have them developed,' warned Becky. 'You really don't have much more time here, do you? I've made all the travel arrangements, and we'll come to the airport to see you off,' she added with more friendliness than she had shown since Kathy had arrived in Holland.

'I'll have to visit Johannes before I go,' said Kathy.

'Of course.' Becky looked surprised. 'I still can't think how you can leave him.'

'Goodnight. I really am tired,' said Kathy, and as soon as she sank into bed she let the hot tears take over and wept as she had never wept since her father had died. The future stretched out over an empty sandy plain when she fell asleep, and she was alone under a hot sun.

She woke to find the sun in her eyes, as she had forgotten to draw the curtains. The morning breeze from the Amstel stirred the pale blue curtains and the delicate, almost transparent folds reminded her of Michiel and Helena and Marijke. Perhaps I would have a better bond of affection with him if I were his patient, she thought wryly. More comfortable. She knew it would never be enough, but at least an exchange of sudden passion for sweet affection would be safe. She smiled. Who am I fooling? I want it all, forever, and so I have to go away, and VSO is the means to do so with dignity.

Michiel arrived at ten-thirty and addressed most of his remarks to Elliot. 'Johannes is feeling fine and has been allowed pillows,' he said. He glanced at Kathy for the first time. 'He says he wants to see you, Kathy. I suggest that you go this evening. I arranged for supper for you at the hospital in his room, as there will be very little time for you to be together before you leave.'

'Thank you,' she said, in a low voice. What was the use of trying to convince anyone that she and Johannes were anything but very dear friends? She picked up her bag and followed Becky to the foyer to watch the two men leave.

Elliot winked at her in passing and said meaningfully, 'Keep Becky occupied, my dear. Can't have her appearing everywhere we go this morning, so Marken is your best bet.' Kathy smiled. Elliot looked like a naughty boy about to do something really mischievous. For a second, Kathy and Michiel looked at each other, the warmth of shared conspiracy over the buying of diamonds bringing them close, then Michiel turned away and opened the door of the car to let Elliot sit in the back seat.

'I'd like to know what he's up to,' said Becky. 'Elliot told me that he loves me, and that when he is really well we must arrange something.' She made a rude face. 'Arrange! If he thinks I'm going to be his mistress with no real security, he can think again. He says he loves me, but he wouldn't say what he was doing today. Did Michiel give a hint to you? I suppose they are visiting yet another broker to buy shares and make even more work for me.'

'Knowing Elliot, I'm sure that you are involved,' said Kathy mildly. 'He's devoted to you, Becky.'

The day passed with a pleasant series of pretty scenes, picturesque people and a very good lunch of grilled fish and wafer-thin pancakes, but to Kathy it was as if she saw it all happening from a distance and had no real part to play in what went on. Becky chatted and bought several pieces of Delft china and some embroidered tray-cloths, and seemed not to notice the fact that Kathy was pale and tense, or if she did she put it down to the fact that Kathy would have to drag herself away from Johannes to go back to England. Some of the lace was fine enough for a bridal veil, and Becky sighed over it and left it reluctantly, slightly annoyed that Kathy didn't share her enthusiasm for white weddings and all the trimmings.

'I've enjoyed today,' said Becky as the taxi took them back over the causeway linking Marken with the mainland. Kathy nodded and found it difficult to speak. Broek in Waterland, by a reedy lake, with its wooden houses and narrow streets, was the kind of place that she would have liked to visit with a lover. She saw the wild fowl rise from the marshes and the sun tracing a path over the water and longed for someone . . . not just anyone, but the one man in her life who would soon fade into her past like a ghost just as the pink-edged clouds lost their form in the breeze and became a memory.

'I'll leave you at the hospital,' said Becky. 'We're later than I planned, but it won't hurt Elliot to wait for me for a change.'

'I'm early for my visit,' protested Kathy. 'I have time

to come back with you.'

'Make the most of it, ducky. I think you are quite mad to go away and leave a sexy hunk like Johannes in a place like this.'

Kathy walked along the hospital corridor slowly. This time there was no urgency, and she was glad to be alone. A nurse in a crisp white uniform eyed her with curiosity and smiled, recognising her as the girl who had come to see Dr Wittener after his accident. There was a hint of amusement in her smile. 'He has had many visitors,' the nurse said when Kathy asked if it was all right to go to his room. 'Very populaire,' she added.

Johannes was propped up on many pillows and looked almost normal, except for the rather dashing white dressing on his head. The bruises were fading, and he now had the appearance of a prize-fighter who had fought and won a fight.

He clasped her hand and she bent to kiss his cheek. 'You look marvellous,' she said. 'I think you were fooling us all the time.'

He laughed. 'I am really better. I shall be able to go to London as I planned and meet your formidable flatmate. I hope you are there, too, and can show me the town.' She shook her head. You have your orders?' She nodded, unable to smile. 'And now it's here, you don't want it?'

She looked away. 'Of course I want to go,' she said. 'I want to go where I can do most good.'

'And you think we don't need you here?'

'I've enjoyed helping out, but I promised to be available and now they need me,' she said, as if to convince herself.

'What is it?' The blue eyes were serious. 'This accident has made me realise that I am not as immortal as I had hoped. A shock makes one know where to go next. I thought I could do without someone to share my life, and now I know that I have been a fool.' He grinned. 'Not you, angel. You and I could never have that special something, could we? Not to last a hundred years.'

'No, but we can be best friends,' she said, and squeezed his hand.

'So why the hollow look behind your eyes, Kathy? Is it Michiel?' She nodded. There was no way she could hide anything from Johannes when he looked at her so gravely. 'He wants you to stay,' said Johannes.

'He wants me to stay and work here because I am efficent and like helping people,' she said bitterly. 'He has no time for me as a woman—at least, not as you said, to last for a hundred years, to marry and have a family.' She shrugged. 'As a one-night stand, perhaps, and I know that I'm old-fashioned, but that's not for me.'

'You made him angry when you thought he might have slept with women like Helena.'

'I didn't say that! He jumped to the wrong conclusion and wouldn't listen. But if she is just a patient, he does seem to see an awful lot of her!' Kathy retorted. 'Most doctors say goodbye to their patients at the clinic door and go on to others who need them more.'

'Be fair, Kathy. There's more to it than that. Hasn't he told you anything of his family?'

'A little,' she said.' He talked about the past, about his sister and his fiancée, but I know nothing of him now apart from his work.'

Johannes shifted on his pillows. 'I saw a picture of Michiel's little sister, the one who died of meningitis when she was about the same age as Marijke, and she *is* very like her. Helena is weak, and could easily lapse into her old ways, but Michiel has arranged lodgings for them, and a woman to care for Marijke if this should ever happen. Helena may marry the man who wants her, but she may not. That is why Michiel has gone to all that trouble to make sure that the child is safe. We can't save all the children here, but we can do our best for some,' he added simply. 'I was very relieved to hear that Michiel had actually succeeded in getting them on that train.'

He hugged her with his good arm. 'Don't cry, my angel. You must learn to give a little, and I don't mean your nursing skills. You have Dutch blood in you, and that might account for your Calvinistic disapproval of all things even slightly immoral. You and he could be good together. Are you completely blind? He wants you very much, little Kathy.'

'But what of love, Johannes? For me, wanting isn't enough.' She hid her face in her hands for a moment to recover her composure. 'It's too late,' she whispered. 'I have to go away, and all that matters now is my work. Soon, I shall be so busy that I may be able to forget that I even came to Holland and met him,' she murmured. 'I shall be gone soon, and maybe in a different country I can forget him.'

'Well, don't forget me, and come back here when you can.' Johannes grinned. 'Are you hungry?'

'No, we had a good lunch,' said Kathy, puzzled at his change of mood.

'Fine! Then you won't need the supper that Michiel ordered for us here.'

'You are turning me out!' Kathy said accusingly, but with a twinkle in her eyes. 'Who is she?'

'Someone I've known for a long time, and tried to forget as I had no intention of settling down.'

'What's for supper? If it's something good, then why should I give it up for some unknown woman?'

'I have no idea, but I promise to buy you the best dinner you've ever had when we meet again, if you'll just go away and leave me to my fate.'

'Really fate? No playing around?'

He swore in Dutch, and then looked resigned but happy. 'No more one-night stands,' he said. 'Besides, it's getting risky, even among friends.'

'Goodbye, Johannes. Be happy.' She kissed him and wished that she could feel this warm friendship for Michiel. It would be so much easier if she weren't in love with him. She left the hospital and walked for a long time, never feeling threatened as she might be in some big cities, reliving the brief moments of ecstasy she had shared with Michiel, but knowing that when she left the city she would never see him again. Music from a brightly painted and heavily carved street organ would remind her, whenever she heard it on a travel programme or in a play where the background was set in Amsterdam. The swift trams would swish through her dreams, but be empty of the man she loved.

She ate *erwtensoep*, the thick pea soup served in so many Brown Cafés in Holland, with fresh bread, and delayed her return to the hotel until she was sure that the others were at dinner, and she could slip into her room and avoid conversation. In the morning, when she was told that the car was waiting for her to go to the airport, she was neatly dressed in a dark blue shirt over a wide print skirt, and Becky remarked that she looked as if she was going on duty and not hastening home to prepare for the adventure of a lifetime.

On the plane, Kathy looked at the literature sent from VSO, and the details of her travel arrangements to the Sudanese border. A little of her former enthusiasm returned, and she was surprised when the familiar outline of the British airport appeared and seat-belts were fastened again.

Michiel didn't say goodbye, she thought as she

retrieved her luggage from the carousel. Becky had given her his message of *bon voyage* and a couple of magazines, and carelessly said that he must be very busy as he, too, was leaving, but Kathy was sure that they would all forget her existence as soon as the plane lifted from the runway. Perhaps Michiel had come to say goodbye after she was in bed, but he had not bothered to telephone in the morning. She shrugged. Who could blame him? He must have known that she was avoiding him, and too much had been said and too much had been left unsaid for them to be at ease with each other ever again.

This time the Customs men waved her through and her bags were not disturbed, and she sank back in a seat on the train to take her to London with a sense that she had never really left England. Red buses, instead of the trams of Holland, and English voices took over, and when she turned her key in the lock she wanted to savour her return and try to regain her love of the city.

She would go back to the Princess Beatrice Hospital and see some of her old friends. She would take a bus and look at all the landmarks that she would not see again for at least two or three years. She stared into space in her room, and wished that her flatmate would come home from work, then remembered that she was away on four nights off, and she would not have been there during the afternoon in any case, as she slept from twelve to seven each day when on a night-shift.

The apartment seemed small after the luxury of the hotel in Amsterdam and, as she packed away her ornaments and pictures ready for storage in the deep cupboard under the stairs that had been cleared for her to use while she was away from the UK, she found old books and clippings that had once meant something, but which now stirred no memories.

She emptied the water from a vase and threw away

the half-dead flowers. The flower market in Amsterdam would be fragrant and dazzlingly bright with every bloom imaginable, and the wet pavements sprayed to keep everything fresh would give up the smell of dust and crushed leaves. She sat on the floor turning the pages of a book about the Sudan, but she saw nothing of the words, and only dimly registered the pictures of the babies and sad-eyed mothers in a camp.

Restlessly, she turned on the radio and heard news of another rail disaster, a military coup in a small republic, and an outbreak of food poisoning in an old people's home. She was about to turn it off when she paused, wishing she had really listened. It was something about the Sudanese border and fighting, but the moment had gone and she was no wiser as to what was happening there.

Kathy returned to her packing and winced as her arm throbbed when she lifted the box containing her books. The last of her jabs against the diseases she might meet in her work in Africa had made her feel lethargic and headachy. She smiled wryly. Michiel had made sure she had every one she needed, and he had certainly given her something to remind her of him—at least until the swollen arm was normal again.

By late afternoon Kathy was feeling worse, and decided to go to bed. She slept until dawn and her head was clear, but she felt wobbly and unsafe to travel far, so decided that she would have to give up a visit to Beattie's and concentrate on feeling fit enough for her main journey. She left the telephone off the hook while she slept all through the next afternoon, and when she woke she suddenly realised that she had eaten nothing for a whole day. Her legs no longer felt like jelly, and she was hungry. The fish and chip shop down the road was a good one, and she dressed and took her purse and keys.

She had put the telephone receiver back before she left, and when she returned the telephone was ringing. The hot package of fish and chips made it difficult to reach her key, and when she opened the door the ringing had stopped. 'Damn!' she said softly. 'That was probably Julia saying when she'd be back.'

She ate supper and watched television, but before the news she switched off, as the antics of the quiz master were too stupid for her in her present edgy state of nerves, and she still had a splitting headache. 'I'm really going away,' she said aloud. 'I am leaving England for two years, and may never come back.'

Slow tears fell as she stood in the shower trying to relax and savour the perfume of her best soap. It was flower-scented and fresh, unlike the heady perfume that Michiel had given her, and yet she found it almost as sensuous. Johannes had said that flower perfumes might suit her better. She tried to imagine the gentle perfume as Michiel's gift.

It was almost as if he caressed her body when the warm smooth bubbles cascaded down her thighs. She shut her eyes, but his face was everywhere, and she dried her hair vigorously as if to rid her mind of his image.

Kathy swathed her head in a towel and answered the phone when it rang again. 'Maria? How nice to hear from you,' she said, pleased that her favourite colleague, the sister-in-charge of Casualty at Beattie's, should remember that she was leaving the country and bother to say goodbye and Godspeed.

'Been trying to get you for days,' said Maria.

'Sorry. Was that you who rang an hour ago? And I did have the phone off the hook for a time, as I wasn't well.'

'No, that wasn't me. What's been happening to you?'

'I've been on a private case in Holland,' Kathy

explained.

Maria grunted and Kathy smiled, imagining her face, as she knew just what Maria thought of private nursing. 'Well, after your nice rest, why not come and do some work for a change? They need a new sister on Out-patients, and at least three of the consultants asked if you would take the job. I said you were going away, but I was asked to tell you the job is free if you can come almost at once.'

'I can't. I have to leave in a day or so, and all the arrangements have been made.' Kathy gulped. 'There's nothing I'd like better, but I am committed. I have the air tickets, my gear packed, and all my jabs are giving me hell.'

'You could get out of it,' said Maria. 'With the news as it is, the Sudan isn't the best place to be just now.'

'That's why they need helpers,' Kathy said patiently. 'If there wasn't trouble, they wouldn't need us.'

'Don't you ever hear the news? Even in Dutch, if that's where you've been? I mean real trouble, with fighting on the borders of the Sudan.'

'I've heard nothing. I would have been contacted if I wasn't to leave,' said Kathy.

'Well, the offer is open for a few days. Ring me before you go, just so that we can advertise or promote someone from Beattie's,' Maria begged. 'I'd rather have you to share my moans, and we have always got on well. One more thing . . .' Maria seemed at a loss for words for once . . . 'we all want you back. Tim has left, and any gossip stopped weeks ago. You just aren't infamous any more, Kathy, so come back and do something useful here.'

'I wish I could,' said Kathy, and meant it with all her heart. Dear old Beattie's, the familiar place with its tradition of care and new research and all that she had taken so much for granted in the past, now seemed the one place on earth where she might be free from Michiel and her terrible need of him, with none of the loneliness she felt when she contemplated life under a Sudanese sky.

She tore off the date on her last day from the desk-calendar, and noticed the motto for the day. 'East, West, Home's best.' How corny can they get? she thought, but felt a lump in her throat. I shall go away alone, with nobody to see me off at the airport, and no one to care when I return—if I ever do. Even Maria had said nothing of waving her off to her new life, and her flatmate was still away. She looked at the card that had arrived that morning, saying that Julia had a virus infection and would be away for at least another week.

Kathy shut the windows and put on the security locks. The bare walls of her room seemed to reproach her, and the stripped bed with the folded duvet and cover was as impersonal as a room in a strange motel. She handed a spare key to the woman in the flat below and wondered when she would see the room again. At least I have bought a share in it, she thought, and it was comforting to know that, whatever happened, she had a place in London that she could call home.

The taxi-driver offered to wait with her luggage while Kathy found a luggage-trolley, and seemed concerned. 'Got a girl about your age,' he said. 'You look a bit peaky, dear. In the club, are you?'

'No, I'm not pregnant. Just suffering from cholera jabs and other nice things they pumped into me.' She thanked him and gave him a generous tip, then pushed the trolley along to the moving platform that led relentlessly to the main hall. Early as usual, she decided. Her father had said that she would be early for her own wedding or her own funeral. She delayed putting her bags through and getting a boarding pass, as this seemed to make the going so much a final and irrevocable step.

The mangled words from the announcer gave news of flights delayed and flights now ready for take-off, and Kathy saw on the board that her flight would not be ready for another two hours. The voice changed and she started. 'Will Miss Kathy Tyler go to the information-desk,' she heard, and it was repeated three times before she realised that they meant her. She pushed the laden trolley before her, and wished that she had left the heavy luggage and obtained her pass, but it was too late now, as a queue had formed and the voice was insistent.

'I am Miss Tyler.' she said.

'Call for you. Take it on that phone,' said the uninterested girl.

'Kathy Tyler here.' She gasped, and listened carefully.

'We sent word to the address you gave in Holland, and tried to contact you personally after Sir Elliot's secretary told us that you had returned to England, but your telephone seemed to be out of order. I hoped that they would contact you if we couldn't, to tell you to stay in England and wait for further orders. They promised to try to get in touch. You haven't booked in, have you?' the anxious voice continued.

'No, I still have my luggage, but why the delay? Do you want me to wait at home until I can go to the Sudan later?'

'I'm sorry if you are all keyed up to go. I know how disappointed you must be, but permission from the Sudanese government has been cancelled due to the fighting and the destroying of two of our main supply camps. I'm afraid we have to cancel your appointment.' There was a pause, then the woman continued. 'I know it's a shock, and there are a number of others besides you who want us to slot them in to another place, which makes things very difficult as we can't arrange new postings for everyone.'

'So you really don't want me?' A hysterical laugh threatened to break Kathy's voice.

'It's not that. Of course we want you, but we shall have to relocate those who have given up jobs to go with VSO.'

'I have a job that I can take up,' said Kathy. Her pulse quickened. 'Please don't worry about me. I'll hand back my tickets, and I suppose I can go home again.'

'Bless you. I wish everyone was as co-operative. If you'd just write to us in about six months' time we may have a firm posting for you.'

'I'll let you know if I'm available,' said Kathy, and put down the telephone. She leaned on the baggage-trolley and saw through a mist the people queuing at the barrier. One man stood at one side, watching the faces of everyone as they filed past, and she caught her breath. The dark hair was as glossy as when she had last seen it in Amsterdam, and the deep cleft in his chin was as endearing—even though he now frowned and looked worried. He spoke to one of the staff, and a minute later Kathy heard her name again over the address system.

'Another goddam late arrival holding up a flight,' growled one American, and Kathy tried to appear small and inconspicuous as once again she went to the desk. The girl glanced up and spoke on a phone link. Kathy stood with her back to the busy lounge and waited, her heart beating fast. He had come to see her off! He was waiting for her, and the girl was giving him a message where to find her. She smiled. He was worried in case he had missed her. Maybe he was only passing through and thought he would say hello and goodbye as he'd missed seeing her on that last evening in Amsterdam, but he did care enough to come here and find her.

'Kathy!' She turned and saw that his eyes were dark with a kind of suffering. 'Kathy, I thought you'd taken that flight.'

'I was due to go,' she reminded him. 'I was told only a little while ago that I was no longer needed, as the border to the Sudan is shut, so they caught me in time.'

'I know about that. I flew over when we couldn't get in touch on the phone.' He glanced at her to see her reaction. 'I had my ticket booked before that, as I knew I mustn't lose you. Somehow, I knew I must stop you leaving, or find a way of joining you out there.' He took her in his arms and the hurrying crowds ignored them as just another couple saying goodbye—or hello—and having no idea of the growing joy and commitment between them in that noisy, impersonal place. The Tannoy commanded and faded, and the trolleys made a background hum of restlessness, but Kathy forgot everything but the man whose arms made her safe from the world. She winced and drew away.

'It's all the fault of your jabs,' said Kathy, with an attempt to sound serious, but her eyes were sparkling. 'I slept and took the phone off the hook, and my arm is still sore.'

'Come on,' he ordered, and she had to hurry to keep up with him. He pushed the trolley as if driving a chariot, and she followed, her breath coming in gasps. They came to the ramp leading down to the car park, and a long dark car slid from double yellow lines and stopped a foot away from the trolley. 'Let's get out of here,' Michiel said, and the driver helped him load the baggage into the boot of the car, then hurried into the airport.

'Who was that?' asked Kathy when she was in the passenger seat and had got back her breath.

'A student from St Thomas's. He wanted a lift, and

I wanted someone to stay with the car, so everyone was satisfied.'

'You went back to Tommie's?'

He negotiated a sharp bend and the car gathered speed towards London. 'I rang them and fixed for someone to bring my car here. There was nothing to make me stay in Holland until my next visit, and the details of the job I applied for came through.'

'What about the clinic in Amsterdam?'

'Hans is back with two assistants who volunteered their help until they get new postings to VSO. You aren't the only one left waiting,' he added. 'I thought you might be really ill when you didn't answer my calls, but I came here straight from my flight to check that you hadn't left before I went to your flat to find you.' He looked anxious. 'Are you all right? When I couldn't get through, I went through hell.'

'I'm better now. My head felt like bursting and my arm throbbed, but a long sleep worked wonders. You did a grand job! It was agony,' she said. 'You didn't have to create havoc in the Sudan just to keep me here!'

He laughed, softly, with relief and something more. 'You can't blame me for the Sudan, but I'm glad you know how much I had to find you again.' He touched her knee briefly, and a thrill of sheer bliss made her blush. 'So you know at last,' he said softly. 'We got off to a bad start, and I hadn't the nerve to tell you that I had followed you and suggested that Elliot might need you as his nurse. When I saw who it was, lying on the floor in a tangled veil of hair, with all that gear on the bed, I was stricken.'

'You remembered me even though we had never spoken to each other?' The wonder of it made her radiant, and she saw his hands tighten on the steering-wheel. He dared not look at her. 'And then you spoiled it by acting as if you might use me as Johannes used women,' she said reproachfully. 'I am not a one-night girl,' she said quietly.

'I thought you were falling for the guy, and I could say nothing. Fool!' he said without rancour, and Kathy wondered if he was referring to the car driver who had just edged in front of them, or if he was bitterly regretting his earlier silence. The tension between them made Kathy clench her hands and make an effort not to touch him. He smiled and relaxed his grip as he glanced at her trembling lips. 'Your place or mine?' he asked as they reached the outskirts of the city. His mouth was curved in an almost permanent smile.

'I'd like to be taken home,' she said.

He laughed. 'Dear Kathy,' he said softly. She glanced at him in profile and her heart was full. His shirt was open at the neck and he had tossed his jacket into the back of the car. He was relaxed and very sure of himself. She tried to avoid physical contact, as each touch seemed to burn into her soul, making her want to be held closely, more closely, and to have him smile like this at her forever. She was still too weak for too much joy.

Kathy recalled how she had left the flat. 'I'm afraid I cleared the fridge,' she said. 'Did you expect to be invited to lunch?'

'No, I thought of that, when I found out your flight number,' was all he said. 'Amazing what you can buy in an airport shop!'

She gave him the key and they brought in the cases and took them into the small hallway. He looked round the tiny sitting-room. 'These, I take it, are your flatmate's things?' he grinned. 'I can't imagine you with pink crinoline ladies and stuffed owls. Not even what I'd expect from your butch flatmate either.'

'I put away everything of mine, as I thought I wouldn't be back for two years.' The enormity of the stretch of time suddenly hit her and her hands trembled. 'Two years. I must have been mad.'

'Two years,' he said, and took her in his arms. 'Two long years, and as soon as you left Amsterdam I knew that I would never let you go. I went through hell wondering if I'd be here in time. I began to believe that Johannes was right.' He laughed softly. 'The old goat has got religion or something. He preached to me about marital bliss, and told me in two languages that I was a fool to let you go. He said that if I was stupid enough to let you out of my sight, then I'd lose you forever.'

They clung together as if saved from a shipwreck, and knew that they had been close to an eternal parting. His kisses were fierce and compelling, and the bare room that had looked like a cell when she left now seemed to expand and become a haven of love and passion. No breeze from the Amstel, no filmy curtains at the window, no romantic music from the street organs, just the buzz of London through the double glazing and the infinite tenderness of their deep emotion. His mouth was searching and warm, his hands gentle but insistent as they traced a prelude to love, taking so much and yet not all, as if the bare room was no setting for the first fulfilment of their desire.

'I brought you a present,' he said when at last they sat fairly demurely at the bare table with the contents of his picnic hamper open and the wine poured.

'Not a pair of clogs or a windmill?' she asked, and wondered if her hair would ever brush into some semblance of order ever again.

'Elliot and I went shopping and the salesman was very persuasive, so I had no chance of getting away without buying some little thing.'

The flash of blue light needed no velvet to show its perfection. Kathy gasped as Michiel took her left hand

and slipped a perfect solitaire diamond ring on to her engagement finger. 'I hope you are old-fashioned enough to believe that this is a promise that will never be broken. Can you ever love me as much as I love you?' he said.

He held her close and she looked dreamily at the ring. 'No tower of tears now. No parting, but I shall remember where I fell in love forever, and I can give you so little in return for this.' He kissed the corner of her mouth and the soft curve of her arched throat. 'Just this, and this, and this, and all our future together,' he whispered. Her body tensed with a delight that flowered beyond her dreams.

She traced the cleft in his chin with one finger, and drew his lips to her breast. Her hands clung to the curling hair at the base of his head, and he lifted her as if she were a rare and fragile wraith and carried her into the bedroom.

'All that I have is yours, forever,' she breathed. 'My love, my life, my future.'

'More precious than diamonds,' said Michiel. He touched her cheek with one finger and a thrill of pleasure made her shiver. She kissed the strong, firm hand and closed the palm over her kiss. '*Now* and forever,' she said shyly, and lifted her face to be kissed, her body soft and as yielding as a cloud, and her eyes full of deep desire and trust. The remains of the meal stayed on the table, and dusk fell while they loved and slept, and woke to make love again, their faces a shadow and their eyes filled with heaven.

Hello!

As a reader, you may not have thought about trying to write a book yourself, but if you have, and you have a particular interest in medicine, then now is your chance.

We are specifically looking for new writers to join our established team of authors who write Medical Romances. Guidelines are available for this list, and we would be happy to send them to you.

Please mark the outside of your envelope 'Medical' to help speed our response, and we would be most grateful if you could include a stamped self-addressed envelope, size approximately $9\frac{1}{4}''$ x $4\frac{3}{4}''$, sent to the address below.

We look forward to hearing from you.

Editorial Department,
Mills & Boon Limited,
Eton House,
18-24 Paradise Road,
Richmond, Surrey,
TW9 1SR.

Mills & Boon

Medical Romances

4 MEDICAL ROMANCES & 2 GIFTS-FREE!

Capture all the excitement, intrigue and emotion of the busy world of medicine - by accepting four **FREE** Medical Romances, a pair of decorative glass oyster dishes and a special mystery gift.

Then, if you choose, go on to enjoy 6 more exciting Medical Romances every two months! Send the coupon below at once to **Reader Service, FREEPOST, P.O. Box 236, Croydon, Surrey CR9 9EL.**

<----------------------- *No stamp required* --------

YES! Please rush me my **4 Free Medical Romances** and 2 Free Gifts! Please also reserve me a Reader Service Subscription. If I decide to subscribe, I can look forward to receiving 6 Medical Romances every two months, for just £7.50 delivered direct to my door. Post and packing is **free**, and there's a free Mills & Boon Newsletter. If I choose not to subscribe I shall write within 10 days - I can keep the books and gifts whatever I decide. I can cancel or suspend my subscription at any time, I am over18.

EP64D

NAME _____

ADDRESS _____

_____

_____ *POSTCODE* _____

SIGNATURE _____

VOWS   *LaVyrle Spencer*   *£2.99*

When high-spirited Emily meets her father's new business rival, Tom, sparks fly, and create a blend of pride and passion in this compelling and memorable novel.

LOTUS MOON   *Janice Kaiser*   *£2.99*

This novel vividly captures the futility of the Vietnam War and the legacy it left. Haunting memories of the beautiful Lotus Moon fuel Buck Michael's dangerous obsession, which only Amanda Parr can help overcome.

SECOND TIME LUCKY   *Eleanor Woods*   *£2.75*

Danielle has been married twice. Now, as a young, beautiful widow, can she back-track to the first husband whose life she left in ruins with her eternal quest for entertainment and the high life?

These three new titles will be out in bookshops from September 1989.

W⬤RLDWIDE

Available from Boots, Martins, John Menzies, W.H. Smith, Woolworths and other paperback stockists.